Most men cheat. As some men cause hur ruthless, conniving, a̲_ _ _ _ _ _ _ _ _ _ _ _ _ _ _ _ _ _ _ destroy the lives of every woman that is unfortunate enough to cross their path. Some women haven't experienced this level of deception. Those women should consider themselves lucky. However, the unfortunate that fall victim to these magicians of trickery and manipulation aren't so lucky. To these women, unfaithfulness is a cake walk. Aaliyah, Tabitha and Jaleesa are examples of these women. Sometimes you can see a man's games from a mile away. Unfortunately, Nas and Moses put much effort in disguising their deception as unconditional love. There is no question that love is presumed to exist somewhere in these relationships. Yet, the drama that comes along with Nas and Moses' love is life damaging, and Aaliyah, Tabitha, and Jaleesa eventually learn that bad men love love too.

Fall into this gritty tale of deception, that goes far beyond petty unfaithfulness and lies, that will leave you realizing that some men simply ain't shit.

FEMISTRY PRESS PUBLICATIONS
Jessica Watkins Presents
A self-publishing entity
info@femistrypress.net
www.jessica-n-watkins.com

Copyright @ 2014 by Jessica N. Watkins

ISBN-13: 978-1500646875

ISBN-10: 1500646873

All rights reserved. No part of this book may be used or reproduced in any manner whatsoever without written permission, except in the case of brief quotations embodied in critical articles and reviews. For additional information, address JWP Publications.

JWP Publications paperback print: August 2014
SBR Publications e-book print: August 2014

Edited by: Femistry Press Editing Services
Cover Design: Trendsetters Publications Inc.

This is a work of fiction. Names, characters, places, and incidents are products of the author's imagination or are used fictitiously and are not to be assumed as real. Any resemblance to actual events, locales, organizations, or persons, living or dead, is entirely coincidental.

Printed in the USA.

If you purchased this book without a cover, you should be aware that this book is stolen property. It was reported as "unsold and destroyed" to the publisher, and neither the author nor publisher has received any payment for this "stripped book".

Thank you for supporting my work.

I pray that you enjoy reading it just as much as I did writing it. Please let me know what you think. I love talking to readers. There is more to come. So, buckle up!

Happy reading!

N.A.S
NIGGAS AIN'T SHIT

JESSICA N. WATKINS

Prologue

Jaleesa

For the first time in days, I had a feeling of joy. I felt good and like things were finally getting back to normal. Life wasn't perfect– not at all. Nevertheless, I had a lot of hope that everything was going to work out.

I practically ran towards my car that was parked half a block down the street.

Once inside of the car, I called Tabitha back as I started the engine. She had called me at least a dozen times while I was in the meeting. She had also sent me a text message asking that I call her as soon as possible.

I wasn't even paying attention when Tabitha answered. I cut her off with excitement as I whizzed through the traffic downtown. "Hey, Tabitha! I know! I'm on my way to the hospital now."

It was like she didn't even hear me. She sounded so out of it as she spoke to me. "Can you come by the house?"

"When? I need to get to the hospital right now. What's wrong?"

"Please, Jaleesa? It's really important."

When I heard the tears, I knew that Nas had done something. I shook my head in irritation and disappointment. I was so fucking sick of Nas and his bullshit. I couldn't understand why he just wouldn't leave that girl alone and let her live.

"Alright. I'm on my way."

She hung up without another word.

"This nigga irks my *soul*," I muttered through gritted teeth as I tossed the phone onto the passenger's seat.

I drove towards the expressway like a mad woman, with hate for Nas fueling my lead foot. Nas was like a thorn in my side. He was negatively affecting everyone's life around him. He was even affecting mine, and I wasn't even fucking him! He was like a virus, slowly eating away at the lives of all us with his inability to give a fuck about anybody else but him.

I thought that Tabitha had finally got the point to stay away from his ass after this last major stunt that he pulled, but apparently not.

Finally, I arrived at Tabitha and Nas' house, completely disgusted that, once again, my life was obligated by Nas or something to do with his ass. I needed to be at the hospital, not at their house consoling Tabitha after whatever stunt he pulled this time.

This better be real fucking important, I thought as I rang the bell. *She better not have called me over here because of some petty shit.*

I repeatedly moved my legs back and forth and stuffed my hands in my pockets to cope with the cold.

It was the beginning of winter, but it was already cold as fuck in Chicago. January was only two days away. That's when the real artic air was going to blow through the city. As I waited for Tabitha to come to the door, I thought about New Year's Eve being the next day. Memories of all that I had been through came to mind, especially the events of the last few weeks. The memories were eerie, but I was happy to start this New Year with hopes of a much better tomorrow.

All of those hopes were lost when Tabitha finally answered the door looking like a walking car accident. Her blond hair was all over the place and hanging in her face. Her eyes were bloodshot red as they rained tears.

When I realized that the stains on her shirt were blood, I lost it. "Tabitha! Oh my God! Are you okay?!"

In response, she turned away from the door and began to mope away. I hurriedly followed her inside, closed the door, and followed closely behind her with a million questions.

"What happened?! Did Nas hit you?! What the hell is going on?!"

"That bitch ass nigga had the nerve to blame me for what happened to Essence!" She fussed with anger while making fast long strides down the hall.

I was on her heels. I was damn near chasing her, confused as she rambled on and on and walked briskly through the house.

"He didn't care! I told him what happened to Essence, and he still didn't care!"

"Didn't care about what, Tabitha?"

She didn't even hear me. "I told him how much I wanted the baby. He just laughed. He dismissed my hurt like it didn't mean anything. He told me that I was overreacting. Told me that all of this was my fault. Told me if I was the ride or die bitch for my man that I was supposed to be, this wouldn't have happened to Essence."

As we entered the kitchen, I still didn't know what was going on. Yet, it was obvious that Nas had finally gone too far. The look in Tabitha's eyes was angrier than I had ever seen before.

She was possessed with fury.

Tabitha was still rambling and crying, nervously running her fingers through her hair.

She sounded like a crazy person. "And do you know what he had the nerve to say?" Her face lost all sanity as she recalled it in her mind. "He said that if Essence wasn't such a hoe like her mother, maybe this wouldn't have happened to her."

Even I cringed as I leaned against the island in the kitchen. "Tabitha, what…"

I stopped mid–sentence when my eyes realized the scene on the floor near the back door.

A gasp escaped my throat so loud that bounced off of the walls. "Tabitha! What did you do?!"

CHAPTER ONE

Tabitha

There was always an afternoon rush at the bank on a Friday afternoon. It was always swarming with customers who'd just gotten paid and needed to make their transactions before the weekend.

This rush was especially hectic because it was only two weeks before Christmas.

"Welcome to Chase. How may I help you?"

I didn't even look up as I closed out the previous transaction while the new customer approached the teller window.

I was tired. I had worked six days straight for twelve hours. Nas, my fiancé, had been busy with the bar and in the studio. He hadn't been able to help me much around the house with the kids lately.

I had two kids. Essence and Eric were thirteen and ten years old at the time, and a complete handful. One would think that since I was only twenty-seven that I would have the energy to keep up with them. Yet, the holiday hours, running around with the kids, and staying up all night, worrying about how we were going to pay the bills and where Nas *really* was, had me delusional, to say the least.

Not to mention, on top of all of that, I was about eight weeks pregnant.

When the customer was taking too long to respond, I frustratingly ran my fingers through my self-colored blond shoulder length wrap. I then looked up, staring down the barrel of a nine millimeter!

I gasped but remained still. Though there was a teller window between us, the gunmen had stuck his slim arm through the circular opening, pointing the gun square at the middle of my forehead.

Too scared to move, my eyes darted from left to right. A few of the bankers were still working on transactions, oblivious to the commotion that was ensuing. A few of the customers had noticed, however. It felt like minutes, but it was only seconds before screams began to fill the air of the small bank on Seventy-Ninth and Western on the South Side of Chicago.

"Nobody move!" The voice was coming from near the front entrance. My eyes darted into that direction. Carl, the security guard, was being held in a headlock by a tall, heavy set guy. Like the guy in front of me, his head was covered with a hood. Every time he moved frantically, as he widely and randomly waved a rifle at the crowd with his other arm, I could vaguely see his eyes.

My eyes darted towards the baritone voice behind the beady discolored eyes of the guy pointing death right at me.

The guy at the door barked, "Hit the mothafuckin' floor!"

And they all did. Like robots, approximately fifteen men, women, and children hit the floor in the lobby, as well as the tellers next to me.

The guy pointing the gun at me started shouting orders at me, "Gimme everything!"

I couldn't believe this shit was happening. I mean, who the fuck still robbed banks in 2014?! This dude couldn't be serious!

"*Now*, bitch!"

Nevertheless, he was *very* serious.

When I saw his finger become much more intimate with that trigger, I moved like a cheetah. I didn't think twice. I wasn't about to lose my life trying to save somebody else's money. I only had two hundred dollars in my own damn bank account. This motherfucker could have had whatever he wanted!

"*Everything*! Her drawer too." He fussed orders at me, but he didn't have to tell me shit. I went from drawer to drawer, opening them and grabbing cash.

By this time, his partner had forced the security guard to enter the necessary code to let him into the back with the tellers. The security guard was sixty years young; too old to fight off a 6'4" oversized, aggressive man holding a glock.

Everything moved so fast, but all of the cashiers just did what they told us to. All of the customers were able to run out of the bank since both of the robbers were in the back with us.

Three minutes went by slowly like three years. Yet, by that time, the gunmen were running out of the security door and back into the lobby, with a garbage bag full of cash.

As I watched them sprint toward the exit, their pants damn near falling with every move, relief left my body with such force that I leaned against the counter and held my head in my hands.

Yet, just as I felt relief, a gunshot pierced the air.

We all screamed and hit the floor just as two more shots rang out. Then the teller window shattered above our heads. I could feel Plexiglas raining down on me.

"Oh my God. Oh my God," I muttered over and over again.

However, just as quick as the chaos started, it was over. The silence in the air was deadly...*literally*.

As we lay on the floor moans of a dying man pierced through the silence.

I could tell by the voice that it was Carl, the security guard.

The only noise heard in the bank was that of Carl, gurgling moans and gasping for air. Though we knew that the gunmen were gone, we all cautiously stood to our feet to make sure. There lay Carl on the ground. His gun was still in his hand. He had two shots to the chest. Blood flowed like a river through his brown uniform.

"Call an ambulance!"

"Oh my God!"

"Jesus!"

"Carl!!"

We were all losing our minds as we ran out of the back and towards Carl. We were five women of different ages and background, but none of us were capable of saving Carl. We kneeled next to him, holding his hand. He moaned, groaned and coughed up blood before he began to slowly lose consciousness.

"No, Carl! C'mon! Don't you die on us," Mrs. Johnson, our shift manager and usher at Reed's Temple Church, said to him as she started to pray.

Unfortunately, it was all to no avail. We watched him take his last breath just as we heard sirens approaching.

Police officers and paramedics rushed in. They forced us to move away from Carl's lifeless body and give them space. We watched them cut away Carl's uniform. Once they did, my coworkers and I gasped at the sight. I could fit my fist in the holes in his chest.

It was too much to stomach. I fought the urge to throw up as the 'inside of Carl's body was exposed by the gunshot wounds.

The police escorted us towards the back as we cried and cringed at the sight 'of Carl's body transitioning to a corpse. There was no use in trying to resuscitate him.

He was gone.

"You ladies have a seat," one of the officers told us. "I know you've been through a lot. But as soon as we ask you some questions, you can leave. Just please be patient with us."

I was happy to be alive, but I was even more irritated that I now had to stay at this motherfucker waiting.

I couldn't even think straight as I headed for my window to get my purse. At the same time, I picked pieces of Plexiglas out of my hair.

After rummaging through my purse, I found my cell. I needed to call Nas. I needed him to pick the kids up for me before the after school program charged me a late fee.

He didn't answer his phone. That was typical. I sent him a text message, asking him to call me as soon as possible. However, I wasn't going to hold my breath.

Nas and I had been together for thirteen years and engaged for one.

I couldn't front; it 'hadn't been no Bey and Jay type of relationship. He got me pregnant while I was a freshman in high school. We were off and on for most of our teenage years, but finally tried settling down once we got in our twenties. I was the only one that settled down though. I never had proof, but I always felt like Nas was cheating. He was always in the streets until early in the morning. He was rarely at home because of one reason or another. But after fourteen years of being with a man, the ups and downs had become routine to me.

He had only proposed to me because I finally caught his ass cheating on me with this random ass bum bitch that lived on his mama's block out West. The bitch had the nerve to send me pictures of his dumb ass sleeping in her bed.

Ignorantly, I allowed the flawed diamonds of the three thousand dollar ring, that he shoved in my face one night while we lay in bed, to persuade me to give him another chance. What was more persuasive was the fact that my need for his half on the bills and his help with the kids trumped me being concerned about some thot that he ran up in at three in the morning.

"You okay, Tabitha?"

I felt Kenyatta's hands on my back. She was the only person that I really fucked with at work. The rest of these chicks were bitter, petty, and messy. Kenyatta was my girl, though. Our gossiping and shit talking helped the work days go by a little bit faster.

"That shit was crazy," I said with a heavy sigh.

People were getting killed every day senselessly in "Chiraq," so we should've been used to stuff like this. However, there was nothing like witnessing it with your own eyes. I was lucky to still have my life after what just happened.

And that's exactly what the police officer told me as he interviewed me fifteen minutes later.

"You're lucky to have your life. Can you tell me what happened?"

I was rambling off my account of what happened while constantly checking my cell. Nas still hadn't responded, so I text messaged my cousin, Jaleesa, and promised to give her gas money for picking up my kids.

"Did the suspects look familiar? Have they been in the bank before?"

I didn't feel like answering this man's questions. I was irritated and hungry! I had a fucking headache!

I knew the officer had nothing to do with any of that, so I calmed down and tried my best to cooperate with him. "Not to my knowledge."

"How did they look?"

"Like a gun! Shit, I didn't see anything but the fucking barrel of a gun in my face! And hoodies. They had on hoodies. The most I saw was dark skin and baggy jeans. I barely saw their faces."

He, Officer Riggins, asked me a few more questions that I couldn't answer before giving me his card and telling me that I was free to go. He told me that they would have more questions for me in the future. I promised to call him if I thought of anything else.

Within seconds I was charging out of the bank without another word. They had already let everyone else go, including Kenyatta.

The scene outside the bank was hectic. People were standing around gaping as the paramedics carried Carl out in a body bag. Squad cars were everywhere. I fought through it all to get to my black 2004 Monte Carlo that sat parked in the back of the lot.

Again, I glanced at my phone, hoping that Nas had called. I wanted something good to eat, not anything in the fridge at home. I was hoping that I could just go home, relax, and have him bring me something to cure my craving.

Yet, Nas still hadn't called.

AALIYAH

"Why does your phone keep ringing, Nas?!"

The admiring smile that Nas then gave his newborn son made me blush. "Stop yelling in front of my shorty."

"Are you serious?" I was beaming. "He's a day old, Nas. He can't hear me."

Nas smiled proudly at his son that I was holding close to my chest. I was performing skin–to–skin. The nurses had me hold my baby while naked, to my bare chest for a certain amount of time ever since he was born last night. I had never heard of such a thing since this was my first born. The nurses said that studies had shown that the skin–to–skin technique had short and long term benefits. I was prepared to do whatever I had to do to make sure that my newborn baby was healthy.

I had lost two babies in the past, so I was extra careful with this pregnancy and my son.

He was my miracle baby.

Nas felt the same way. He sat beside my hospital bed in a big leather chair looking at us with the biggest smile on his face.

"What are we going to name him?"

"*Shiiid*," he cursed as he looked like I should know the answer to that already. "His name is Nasiem, after his daddy!"

I giggled because I knew that would be Nas' answer. Because of Nas' Muslim name, his baby mama, Tabitha, hadn't named his firstborn son after him. She was raised Christian and did not want her kids having Muslim names. Nas had never really gotten over that. Obviously Nas didn't practice the Muslim faith like his parents, but he still held those traditions close to his heart.

"Okay, baby. He'll be Nasiem Shiraz Ramli, Jr."

To see Nas sitting there with so much pride in his eyes gave me such a feeling of joy.

I loved me some Nas. I met him on a video shoot. I had been doing some eye candy modeling on the side for a few months when I got a call from my cousin, Lisa, one day. Lisa and I weren't that close growing up. She lived in Indianapolis. However, when her baby's father, Carlos, told her that his best friend, Nas, was shooting a video for his artist, Moses, she recommended me to fill one of the eye candy roles. Since I was familiar with Moses and his music, I knew that the music video wouldn't give me much exposure. But he was a hit in the hood, so I did it anyway. It ended up working out more for me than the two hundred dollars I was paid for showing up. It was me and three other big bubble butt chicks with missing waists on set, but Nas kept his eyes on me. I couldn't resist a man like him. His presence put me under a spell. He had the height of an NBA player but wide build of an NFL player. His full neatly trimmed facial hair and chocolate skin gave him such a grown man swag. But his Trukfit apparel showed that he was still a street nigga.

After the video shoot, we hit the after party at the bar that he owned on the South Side; The Black Room. I had actually been there a few times, but I couldn't believe that I had never seen him there before. We partied and popped bottles until four in the morning. Needless to say, we got a room that night and passionately, yet vulgarly, rode each other as the sun came up.

That was a year ago. We had been together ever since.

Nas was my beau. He spent a lot of time at the bar and trying to get Moses a deal with one of the big labels. Yet, my baby always came home to me and took good care of me. I wasn't flossed in the most expensive labels or diamonds, but I barely had to lift a finger while I spent my days going to cosmetology school and tending to the house that we bought six months ago. I stopped modeling once Nas and I got serious, a little over nine months ago when I found out that I was pregnant. He didn't like other men seeing me half naked, so he convinced me to do something else with myself. I then started cosmetology school and got a job as a receptionist at Kenwood

Retirement Home. Nas was going to buy me my own shop as soon as I got my license.

I didn't blame him for molding me into a more mature woman; out of the booty shorts, into slacks, and into a real career. I was twenty–three at the time, and he was thirty. He was older and knew better, so I always listened to my man.

He was a bit of a control freak, and you couldn't tell him shit. Yet, I appreciated a man that could lead and had enough self–esteem to do so.

I loved everything about Nas. I thought he was my end all and be all. Sitting in that hospital with him and our child was a dream come true. It felt so right.

Nobody could have convinced me otherwise.

Nobody could have made me believe how far left things were going to go after that day.

NAS

Now that I had made my way out of the hospital, I ran through the parking lot while dialing Tabitha's number. I hadn't talked to her, but the shit was all over the news. I knew she was pissed that I wasn't answering. I was right next to Aaliyah, so I couldn't answer Tabitha's calls. When I had a free moment, I was busy text messaging Nell, making sure that everything had gone according to plan.

Things had gone the total opposite of the fucking plan though. Them stupid motherfuckers were supposed to get cleanly in and out.

Not commit felony murder!

"Nas, where the fuck have you been?!"

As expected, Tabitha was pissed when she answered the phone. I cringed as she tore my head off while I sped out of the parking lot of the University of Illinois Hospital.

"I've been calling you all fucking day…"

"Baby, wait…"

I tried to calm her down, but she couldn't even hear me over her own nagging, ranting, and raving. "The bank got robbed today! This man came to my window and pointed a gun at me!"

"Tabitha, calm …"

"I had a gun to my head, and you wouldn't even answer the fucking phone!"

"Baby, I know. That's why I'm rushing home right now. My mama just called Nell looking for me because she saw the news. I've been with Nell all day. My phone was in his car. We've been in Indianapolis all day."

She would believe that. My closest homeboy, Carlos, had a crib in Indianapolis that we escaped to from time to time. He sold major weight from Chicago all the way to New York.

Sometimes we went to Indianapolis to get away from the many phone calls and interruptions of the street life.

Tabitha sighed heavily before she asked, "When will you be home?"

"We just left. Its gon' take about three hours to get to the crib."

That was about all the time I needed to get back out south, get the cash from Lavell, Nell, and Caine, and make it to the crib.

Tabitha smacked her lips hard. I imagined her eyes rolling in the back of her head just as hard. But like a good little girl she was going to be cool with it.

Tabitha wasn't a stupid chick, by any means. She had her shit together the best way she could, considering the hand that she was dealt. I knocked her up when she was fourteen. She was pregnant again by her senior year. She was a good kid. She was an honor roll student. Hell, she was even in the band. Even after having Essence, she kept her grades up. But once my son was born, going to college with two kids just wasn't in the cards for her. Having to get a job at some fast food restaurant devastated her, but she quickly worked her way up to a management position. Then she was blessed with a job opportunity at Chase bank about two years ago.

Tabitha's problem was me. I didn't love her. I don't think I ever did. I felt stuck with her since I knocked her up the first time. For years, I played the role of the family man. I even put a ring on it. My heart had never been in that relationship though. My heart, my love, was making it big.

I always wanted to be the richest nigga in the hood, flipping hundred thousand dollar cars with fly cribs all over the city. As a kid, I hustled for years, but my inability to manage my money between kids, women, and stunting had prevented me from ever elevating to that status.

I'd dropped out of CVS High School before Tabitha even got there her freshman year. While she was getting good grades in school, I was standing outside causing trouble. I was never really into selling drugs. I was a thief. From cars to electronics, I stole everything.

I never had any intentions of being in school or working. Being in the streets was all that I ever wanted to do, until I decided to stop putting my life in danger. I took the money I had and bought The Black Room. The money that I made from the bar was cool, but it wasn't enough. I wanted the high life with foreign vehicles and lavish homes. Not a baby mama, two kids, with a one–story brick house on the South Side, and a side bitch with good enough credit to get a crib that I actually liked; all of which I struggled to pay for with bar money.

Life felt real regular until I started managing my cousin Moses. That lil' nigga was a beast. I would hear him flowing with his friends when I went to my Aunt Tina's house. I kept telling him that I was going to make him a star. I put a lot of my money into Steve, who I gave the stage name Moses, because his gutter street flow spoke to the audience like a prophet. We had been at this shit since he was eighteen. For the last two years, things were slowly progressing. He was a hit in the streets. He did shows here and there. We had a few low-budget videos on YouTube that had a lot of hits, resulting in his music popping up on a few mixtapes. His music had taken over the schools. The shorties loved the violence and ratchetness of his lyrics.

I just needed to get him popular outside of the hood, because if he got on, so did I.

With this money from the robbery, I could do that and then some. I would finally be the man in my mind that I made everyone think I was. I was always that dude that demanded attention from the ladies and obedience from niggas around me. With this money from the robbery, I would finally be on for real and be able to shift Moses' rap career into full speed.

For years, I never could figure out a way to get ahead for good, but *this* was it.

Had I told Tabitha what I was planning, she would never have gone along with it. So I continued to milk her for information about the bank, while nonchalantly getting my own surveillance when dropping off money or lunch for her. Since I was her man, security was always lenient with me.

"Hello?"

"Hey baby." Aaliyah sounded exhausted. I could hear Nasiem crying in the background. "When are you coming back?"

"In a few hours. The receptionist at the front desk said that she would let me back up if I get back after visiting hours. You hungry? I'm headed out South."

"Ooo! Yea! Bring me some steak tacos from Fred and Jack's."

"Bet."

I hung up, biting my lip in frustration as I tried to figure out how in the hell I was going to get out of the house without Tabitha having a fit.

There wasn't a deep explanation as to why I was playing these women. I wasn't torn between the two at all. It was simple; I wasn't shit. That's just the type of man that I was. I loved being with women and more than one. The attention was exhilarating. I wasn't in love with either of them. However, I was passionately in love with how they served me. I felt like the man having women at my beck and call, loving me and holding their breath until the moment I graced them with my presence.

Ever since I was young, I had been juggling multiple women with ease. It was a powerful feeling to be needed and adored by so many women. I was so madly in love with having so many hearts at the tip of my fingers that I did whatever I could to romance my way into their hearts just to keep that feeling of power over them.

Relationships had always been a game of control.

And I always won.

CHAPTER TWO

Jaleesa

I was wide awake when I heard Moses creeping through the house at five o'clock in the morning.

I could hear the front door creaking leisurely as if he was slowly opening it. The rubber of his Timberlands made slow, sticky sounds as I imagined him creeping into the house. When I heard him sit on the couch, I jumped out of bed.

"Oh hell nah." I fussed and growled as I made my way into the living room.

Barefoot and wearing a pair of my old high school gym shorts, a sports bra, and a satin cap, which kept me from sleeping on my weave, I whisked into the living room so fast that Moses didn't even see me coming.

"Where you been, Moses?!"

At first, he jumped at the sound of my voice. Then he tried to play it off like he had no worries. He casually asked me, "What you doin' up, man?"

Then he had the nerve to lay back on the couch like he was in the right!

I approached the back of the couch and nudged the back of his head. "Don't play with me, Moses!"

"C'mon, man," he whined. "Chill before you wake the baby up."

Our "baby" was three years old. Trenton was the spitting image of his average height, light skinned, scrawny ass daddy. Moses was attractive because of his bad boy image, the locs that hung low to his waist, and monstrous dick game.

I flopped down next to him on the couch so hard that he was forced to sit up and move out of my way.

"Where have you been?! And don't say the studio, because I called and checked. You weren't there! And you weren't with Nas either! Tabitha already told me."

Ever since Moses started getting all this street fame, this shit was going to his head. He was no longer the humble man that loved and adored me and his son. All of a sudden he developed this don't–give–a–fuck attitude and started disrespecting me. I had never caught him cheating, but I had a gut feeling that he was doing more than staying in the studio rapping over beats all night.

"Bae, chill," he had the nerve to say with a giggle. "I was just chillin' with my homeboys."

I smacked my lips, rolled my eyes, and mocked him with anger as I stood up. "*With my homeboys.* Whatever, Moses!"

With a smile, he tried to grab my shorts, but I jumped out the way and smacked his hand away. "You playin' but I'm serious! I'm sick of this shit! Being in the studio is one thing, but this shit is getting out of hand. You haven't been home all fucking day! I been at school, at work, running around after Trenton, and you been kickin' it! Were you out there getting money for the rent? 'Cus it's past due."

Suddenly, his haughty attitude disappeared. "I told you Nas said he would lend it to me."

I waved my hands in the air dramatically. As they landed hard against my thighs, I asked, "Why Nas gotta pay the rent, Moses?! What are *you* doing? I'm the only one in the house busting my ass. I'm sick of it!"

With frustration, Moses cupped his forehead. "Look, I need to get some sleep. I gotta go see my probation officer in the morning."

As I stomped away, I heard him ask, "Can I use your car?"

Tuh, I thought to myself as I reached the bedroom.

Before slamming the door, I shot back, "Hell nah!"

On top of the ever present bullshit, Moses was on probation. He had been arrested multiple times on weapon and drug charges, resulting in being convicted of many misdemeanors and two felonies. However, he had only been sentenced to probationary periods because, like the state of his pockets, his crimes were petty.

I was so sick of this shit. Much worse than the possibility of him cheating on me, Moses was always broke, getting on my nerves, and going to court. When my cousin, Tabitha, first introduced me to her man's cousin, Steve, I was head over heels. Like I said, his bad boy image was enticing to a young girl from the hood. We were like two peas in a pod.

Over the four years that we'd been together, things had changed. I was no longer the teenage girl that was cool with standing on the block with her man all day, barely making it. I had matured into a woman that was going to college, working, and taking care of her son. I didn't have much, but an apartment on the South Side of Chicago and a used 2010 Expedition that I was barely making the payments on, but I was tired of busting my ass to make it when there was a well and able–bodied grown ass man laying up in my house.

Moses was cool with living off of weed money until he made it big– *if* he made it big. His videos had hundreds of thousands of views on YouTube. His mixtapes were selling well in the streets. He even had some downloads on iTunes. Nas was even booking him a few shows here and there. But, since he was just a local rapper, none of the shit was paying the bills! And since Nas kept convincing him that he would soon be this big star, Moses wasn't trying to hear me when I attempted to convince him to get a job so that he could help out more around the house.

I was only putting up with this shit for one reason. If by some miracle he did make it to being this big famous rapper, *I* was going to be the bitch by his side. I had put in the work. I deserved to be the chick on Instagram flossing in diamonds, foreign cars, and Giuseppe. I deserved to be with him at the BET awards.

Not some random chick.

I was so upset! As I lay in the bed, all I could think about was how I had to come up with the rent money in a few days. I didn't get an ounce of sleep before my alarm went off at eight o'clock, notifying me that it was time to get ready for work. As I got dressed, I avoided the living room at all costs. It was too early in the morning for another altercation with Moses, so I regretted having to go in there to get Trenton ready, since I could hear him in there watching cartoons.

"Trent, where is your daddy?"

Trenton was sitting on the couch where I had last seen Moses. I had been in other parts of our two–bedroom apartment, so I knew that Moses wasn't anywhere else.

"He left."

"Left?! Where did he go?"

In his raspy, three–year–old voice, he told me, "Him said him had to go to probation."

I cringed at the fact that my baby even knew what probation was. I blamed myself for his early knowledge of such a street life.

I flew towards the window, only to see a big empty space where I parked my truck last night.

"*Fuck*! Stupid motherfucka!"

"Mommy, you cussed."

"I'm sorry, baby," I mumbled as I stumped out of the living room. I continued to grumble as I went into the bedroom looking for my phone. "Can't believe this, nigga!"

I called Moses a few times, but got no answer. Usually, he had to be at probation by eight. And as I remembered correctly phones weren't allowed. It was after eight, so I gave up. Regretfully, I called my girl, Tia. She worked with me at the Target on Eighty–Seventh and Cottage Grove. We were cool outside of work as well. We hung out from time and time. We'd grown close enough that we vented to each other about our men. So, she was also just about as tired of Moses as I was.

"Hello?"

My eyes rolled into the back of my head. I hated to even have to ask her this. "You left for work yet?"

"Just about to. Why? What's up?"

"I need a ride," I said with a heavy sigh as I slipped on the black gym shoes, which went along with my Target uniform. "Moses took my fucking car without telling me." As soon as she smacked her lips and was getting ready to go in, I stopped her. "I know! I know! You don't even have to say anything. I am so sick of this shit, girl."

Of course, as friends do, she told me about myself anyway. "I can't tell. This nigga is always putting you in a bind. You steady busting your ass trying to work to keep your lights on, fixing these little problems, when *he's* the bigger problem. It's one thing after another that you have to deal with or fix because of this nigga. Stop swatting at the flies and get rid of the shit. And *he* is the shit!"

TABITHA

"I don't want to do this, Nas."

I was fighting back tears as Nas and I rode the Dan Ryan towards downtown.

He didn't respond. All I could hear was Moses' voice. Nas always played Moses' music.

"Nas, listen to me," I said as I turned the radio down.

He kept his eyes on the road, totally avoiding the pain in my eyes.

I had gone through so much the night before that I woke up the next morning remembering that I had to go to the clinic. I didn't want to go before the robbery, but I definitely didn't want to after what I'd just experienced.

Life was so precious.

"I don't want to do this, Nas," I reiterated with pleading eyes.

He simply said, "I'm not ready for another kid," while keeping his eyes on the expressway.

"*Please* don't make me do this, Nas. I don't mean any disrespect when I say this, but why do *you* have to be ready? You're hardly home with the kids anyway. I'm the one at home with the kids all day. So having this baby would be on me, not you."

"And on *my* pockets," he answered without looking me in the eyes.

While I had been successful in not crying like a baby before, what he just said made the tears fall along with sobs. I saw the disappointment in his face when he heard me crying. I wasn't trying to be a brat. I just honestly wanted to have my baby. I know that I already had two, but my kids were older. I felt like at the age of twenty-seven if I didn't have another child then, I probably never would. I had never experienced having a baby and being happy about it. Essence and Eric were mistakes; beautiful mistakes, but mistakes nonetheless. There was no celebration, no congratulations, and no baby showers. There was only scolding from our parents for having babies so early.

I felt like this baby was my last chance at having a happy pregnancy. This was our chance at experiencing a happy birth of one of our children and raising it right. We had finally gotten to a place where we could afford to live and get our kids what we wanted. I wanted to be able to give our child what the first two were a few years shy of.

When I found out that I was pregnant with this baby, I actually smiled. That had never happened to me before. Every time that I had gotten pregnant before, it was a depressing realization because, at first, I was too young to have a baby. Then I knew that Nas wasn't ready for more kids. Yet, he kept fucking me recklessly as if we would just keep fixing the problem with three hundred dollars.

The timing was perfect this time. Now we were engaged to be married. Moses' career was looking good. Money wasn't spilling out of our pockets, but if we could make it happen with two kids, I didn't see why we couldn't make it happen with three.

"Baby, just give us a little more time." Finally, he let his guard down and revealed the man that I loved. As he spoke to me, he reached towards me and gently held my hand. "I promise I plan to give you and my kids everything that you want as soon as I can make the moves that are in motion. This just isn't the right time. I promise to make it up to you. I love you to death. Of course, I want to have as many kids as I can with the love of my life. This just isn't the right time."

When he lifted my hand to his mouth and kissed it, I let it go.

Ironically, I appreciated the love that I felt right then. Between how much I worked, the kids, and how much time Nas spent at the bar and the studio, we didn't spend much alone time together. And though we were on our way to a somber moment, having him there to hold my hand was the most intimate moment we'd spent together in a long time.

NAS

Between wiping Tabitha's crocodile tears all night and sneaking back to stay the night with Aaliyah, I never made it to holler at Nell, Lavell, and Caine after they hit the bank. But we were heavy on text securing a spot to stash the cash from the robbery. Now I was on my way to meet up with them after dropping Tabitha off at the crib.

I felt a hell of a lot better now that she wasn't pregnant anymore. One more kid just wasn't in the cards for a playa. Hell, it wasn't in the cards for me nine months ago when Aaliyah got knocked up, but, after having two miscarriages, I couldn't talk her into going to the clinic for shit.

Tabitha needed to focus on the two kids that she had anyway. Essence was in her teens, and she was blossoming into her mother's physique. I'd caught her and guys on the block giving each other googly eyes and shit. Eric was clumsy as fuck. Every other week he was bleeding from somewhere or breaking something. He stayed in the emergency room.

Tabitha didn't need any more kids right now; she needed to keep an eye on the ones she already had.

"Man! Pops, you need to wrap that thang up," Caine told me with a laugh as I showed him pictures of Nasiem.

Me, Caine, and Nell were at Caine's spot out in Lansing. It was actually his mom's crib. Lavell couldn't come through because he had to take care of shit with his baby's mother.

I met Caine and Lavell a few months ago through some homeboys. Eventually, they asked me to give them some work at the bar so they could make some bread. Though we were the same age, they both looked up to me like little brothers; like I was daddy. They were those kinds of niggas that never really did anything for themselves. I used them as security at The Black Room just so they could have a couple dollars in their pockets. Nell was in the same predicament, except he was my cousin. That's why when I told them about hitting that lick at the bank. They was all for it, for little or nothing. I promised them a small cut in exchange for doing the dirt for me.

They were only able to get roughly thirty thousand out of that bank though. So after giving them their cut, I was left with about twenty g's. Not enough to do anything but pay off some bills at the bar and have a little left over. At this point, the robbery seemed worthless. Sure enough, I could eat off of twenty thousand dollars for a minute. The holidays would go over a hell of a lot smoother now. The point wasn't to eat though. It was to floss. Not much flossing was possible with a measly twenty thousand dollars. I was forced to put it to the side until I came up with another scheme to get more cash.

"My bitches ain't dippin' off on me," I said slyly as I slid my phone back in my pocket. "I ain't gotta wrap shit up. They do need to get on some birth control though."

Caine simply shook his head at me.

"What I need to know is how in the hell y'all left out of there with only thirty thousand?!"

Caine shook his head again, as if he was disappointed in that as well. Nell walked out with a chuckle, since he didn't have anything to do with that. He was outside waiting in the driver's seat of the getaway car when it all went down.

"Them bitches was movin' slow as fuck," Caine told me. "We didn't have time to get to where the real money was. We had to get out of there fast, man!"

With frustration, I shook my head just as Nell walked back in with my cut of the cash secured in bundles wrapped in rubber bands.

"Put it in a bag or something, fam! You want me to walk around with this shit?!" I shook my head, in disbelief of his stupidity. "Stupid!"

They were stupid. All of them. They were peons. They didn't have the knowledge to do anything for themselves. That's why they depended on me. And that's how they ended up with a murder on their hands all for a measly couple grand a piece.

"Now, how the fuck y'all end up killin' that dude?"

"Man, we was on our way outta there and he just started shootin'! I had to pop back," Caine said defensively.

Handing me a fake Gucci duffle with the cash in it, Nell nodded in agreement. "He's right, fam. I was watching through the doorway. They were on their way out of there, and the old man pulled his piece. I couldn't believe that shit. Buddy was on some super cop shit."

The robbery had been all over the news. Luckily, the security cameras didn't get a shot of their faces. I told them to set the car on fire that they were riding in last night. As far as we could tell from the news coverage, the police didn't have any suspects. But I would know more once Tabitha took her ass back to work.

Either way, if they got caught, it was on them. I wasn't there. That's why I set the shit up like that. Regardless, they were so loyal to me, the man that fed them, that they would never snitch.

Either way, I was good.

CHAPTER THREE

TABITHA

I had been in a serious funk for the past two days. I had never felt this way after terminating a pregnancy. I was constantly on the verge of tears. I was so depressed. I just couldn't shake the feeling.

I really wanted that baby. I *really* did. However, as I got the kids together for school that morning, and myself together for my first day back to work, I couldn't imagine having to get a newborn ready as well. Nas had left quite early that morning to take care of some things at the bar, so I was there alone, fussing with kids that didn't want to go to school.

"Shut up! Damn!" I yelled at Essence as she pouted about her hair not looking right. "It's your last day of school before Christmas Break anyway!"

Essence looked at me like I had lost my mind. I felt like I kinda had. I was just irritated about everything. Nas was right. The time wasn't right, but I really wished that it was.

"You probably have postpartum depression," Kenyatta told me once I got to work.

"Huh? I thought women only got that after having a baby."

"You *were* pregnant. Even though you terminated the pregnancy, maybe your hormones are just out of whack. Or *maybe* you just really wanted your baby, Tabitha. And now you regret letting Nas talk you into getting an abortion."

I sighed as I leaned against the counter. Kenyatta and I were whispering since we were the only other tellers there besides Jay, with his fine ass. As usual, he was all into his phone since the bank was empty. Outside of being a teller at Chase, he was a party promoter. He stayed on his phone promoting his nightlife events on social media.

It was early on a Monday morning, which was usually a slow day for us. Yet, for it to be merely a week before Christmas, the lobby was surprisingly a ghost town. The whole neighborhood had heard about the robbery, so customers were avoiding this bank like the plague.

Hell, I didn't want to be there either. The manager's had beefed up security, though. Now there were two undercover cops in the lobby.

"Tabitha, can I see you in my office for a minute?"

I hid my frustration as the branch manager Frank stood at the door waiting for me to follow him. I could only imagine what he wanted. He probably had his own questions about the robbery. We hadn't been able to talk since it happened. I didn't really feel like reliving that shit. Not that day. Not any day. I just wasn't in the mood.

"Have a seat, Tabitha," he told me as he gestured toward the blue leather chair across from his desk.

As I sat, I felt horrible cramps in my pelvic area. I felt like complete shit, both emotionally and physically.

"As you know, it's that time of year when we perform employee annual evaluations. I've been monitoring your work performance. You've been late to work quite a few times."

This didn't sound good. As he spoke, he avoided my eyes. I cut him off right there. "I understand that I have been late quite a bit, Frank. I do have two children, so I have had a few emergencies here and there."

The emergencies were Nas' lack of help. I was constantly late for or leaving work because he couldn't pick the kids up or go to the school for one thing or another. He was always so tied up with Moses' career and the bar that I was basically a single parent. Not to mention all of Eric's freak accidents. I was constantly running out of work after calls from the school nurse telling me that Eric was on his way to the ER.

I swear that boy had two left feet.

"We all have children, Tabitha."

It took a lot for me to bite my tongue. I wasn't in the mood to have a motherfucker coming at my head about what I was not doing and how I was not good enough.

I already felt like that.

"And your customer service skills aren't up to par."

Now he was just picking me apart.

With a face full of confusion, I asked, "Have you gotten complaints from any of the customers?"

This felt like a sudden attack. I hadn't been reprimanded before about these things. Many of my coworkers were late and gave the customers attitude without being hauled into his office.

I didn't understand why he was being so critical all of a sudden.

Frank answered my question by saying, "Unfortunately, we are going to have to end your employment here."

I couldn't even hide my shock. "Are you serious?!"

"Unfortunately, yes, Tabitha."

"Does this have something to do with the robbery? Frank, I had to give that man what he wanted. They had guns! They killed Carl! They would have killed me!"

His face was blank as he mechanically replied, "I'm sorry, Tabitha. This is out of my hands."

"How am I going to take care of my kids?"

I was really talking to myself, but Frank looked at me like he couldn't care less. "I'll give you the opportunity to gather your things. Please turn in your ID before you leave."

I felt like I had been punched in the stomach. I didn't even bother to hide the tears as I stood to leave. I needed this job. Well into his thirties, Nas had hood dreams that had yet to come to fruition. We had a roof over our head and lights because of me. Nas claimed that the bar wasn't getting enough business, so money wasn't coming in like it used to. Without this job, we were going to struggle.

I defiantly slammed the door behind myself after leaving his office.

"Tabitha, you okay?"

I couldn't even respond to Jay as I walked towards my window to get my things. Kenyatta looked at me with concern as I grabbed my purse.

She asked, "Did he fire you?"

All I could do was nod. She hugged me. She knew how bad I needed that job. That job was the only thing that I had accomplished. I worked hard to get to that position, considering that I had never been to college. It was the one thing that I was proud of; the one thing that I did right.

AALIYAH

Now that Nas was gone to the bar, I had the opportunity to clean up the house a little bit. He'd come in at about seven in the morning, after leaving the studio. Between cooking breakfast for him and tending to the baby, I was beat. I had only been home from the hospital for a day. But I liked to keep a clean house for Nas. I took good care of him – feeding him, fucking him, sucking him, and keeping a clean house – because he took good care of me. He was paying all of the bills while I was in school.

I was barely making it as I vacuumed the living room. My stomach was killing me. The post birth cramps were a bitch. I decided to finish up vacuuming and take it easy. I needed to make sure that I felt good enough that weekend to party. Friday was Moses' birthday party at Billboard Live.

As I pushed the leather couch away from the wall in order to vacuum behind it, I was startled by the sight of a Gucci duffle bag. That's where Nas' stash was that he thought I knew nothing about. Though he had a legit business now, he still thought like a street nigga. He had no bank accounts and hid his money. I often slipped money from the stash when he was being stingy. He barely noticed.

However, this Gucci bag looked like it belonged to a woman. I knew damn well that it wasn't mine, so I instantly turned off the vacuum and went for it. When I opened it and saw all of the money inside, I figured that it must have been Nas'. But where he got the money from was news to me. From what he told me, the money he made at the bar wasn't like *that*. He had been claiming that he couldn't afford any more kids, but it looked like about twenty thousand dollars inside that bag.

Once again I was startled, but this time by the sound of someone coming through the house. I tried to quickly zip the bag back up, drop it and push the couch back against the wall.

"What up, Aaliyah?"

Luckily, it was Nas' brother, Fabe. I still didn't want him to know that I knew where Nas' stash was, though. I hoped that he hadn't seen me behind the couch as he entered the living room.

I left the back door open a lot. Nas, his brother, or one of his friends were always coming in and out. We lived on a nice block on the southwest side of Chicago, in Beverly, so I felt safe enough to leave it open.

"Hey, Fabe. What are you doing here?" I tried to act nonchalant as I wrapped the cord around the vacuum. "Nas just left."

"I saw him," he told me as he walked towards me. "I came in to check on you."

The closer he walked towards me, the further I backed into the couch. Eventually, I had to sit on it. He sat snugly beside me with his arm around me. Instantly, my heart started to race.

After a year of being around him, Fabe still made me nervous.

He was so fine. He was the complete opposite of Nas. I loved my man to pieces and he was fine as shit too, but Fabe had a sophisticated, romantic swag about him that made my pussy wet, just by the sight of him, real talk. That's why last year, around the time that Nas and I first met, Fabe was able to talk me out of my panties and had me bent over in his Benz truck giving me the complete business. I had just met Nas, so he and I weren't officially a couple yet. We were all drunk and leaving The Black Room. Nas told me that he would meet me later that night at my apartment. After he drove off, Fabe pulled up next to my car. He looked at me and dared me to deny the chemistry between us. I abandoned my car and slipped into the passenger side of his truck. An hour later, I had cum four times.

But once I sobered up, I realized that that romantic swag was not worth me losing Nas. Fabe was smart, legit, and college educated. He was an accountant at some company downtown. He was a nice, regular guy who lived a regular life out in the burbs. A girl like me wasn't meant for a man like him. Nas was a street nigga, and the streets raised me. He was on my level, and vice versa. We meshed well.

Fabe felt some type of way afterwards as well. He avoided Nas for weeks. When he eventually started to come back around two months later, I was deep in love with Nas. Therefore, it was fairly easy for me to ignore the way Fabe would attempt to flirt with his eyes when Nas wasn't looking and whisper sweet nothings into my ear when Nas wasn't around. If I wanted to fuck him again, I could have. However, I loved Nas more than I wanted the dick.

When Fabe was around, I tried to ignore the undeniable chemistry. I told myself to forget about the few hours we shared having probably the best sex of my life. But what I could not ignore was the fact that I didn't even feel that type of intimacy with Nas.

The simple sound of his voice made me leak with memories of his voice against the nape of my neck as he told me to cum. "How you been?"

And that's how he always was. He was always so caring and wanted to know about me. Behind his eyes, I could always see that he wondered if I thought about that night.

NAS

I was in my office in the back of The Black Room chillin'. I was finalizing plans for Moses' birthday celebration when Fabe walked in.

First thing he said was, "Your girl found your stash, bro."

"How you figure?"

He sat down next to me wearing a polo and jeans, his normal fit that he wore to the gig.

Me and my brother were polar opposites. With different mothers, we were raised differently. But his strict upbringing led him to sneak to visit the hood and hang with his big brother often. Luckily his time with me didn't change the man that he grew into. While he matured and went to college, I was still on the block. Now he was in cargo pants at a nice gig making decent money, and I felt like I was still trying to make it.

In all honesty, he had the better hand. He had his shit together and was working hard to save money to open his own barbershop. He even worked as an accountant on the side for me at The Black Room. He was a better man than me, but I would never let him know that.

One thing that we had alike was love and loyalty for family. He knew I was a hood nigga and respected that part of me. He never told anyone about the things I shared with him that I did to get money when we were shorties. When I needed his college education to help me pull off that robbery, he was there for his big bro.

"When I came through looking for you, she was behind the couch. Better fix that shit. I'm sure she went back behind there when I left. She might wonder where you came up with twenty g's."

"Her dumb ass ain't gon' know."

Fabe looked at me like I was a heartless son of a bitch. I didn't bother denying it. I could tell Aaliyah anything to send her off, and she would believe it.

Not because she was stupid. She just trusted and loved me that damn much. Too much, if you asked me. But that is exactly where I wanted and needed her to be.

Shaking his head at the smug, arrogant look on my face, Fabe gave up on the subject. "What's up with Moses' party? You ballin' out and buying bottles now that you got that paper?"

"I can't spend that paper for a minute. Bills are marked. Gotta sit on it for a minute until I can change that shit out," I explained. "But that party gon' be dope. Got VIP on lock, and he's performing."

Since The Black Room was too small to hold the crowd expected at Moses' birthday party, I had to have his party at

Billboard Live. Luckily Carlos sold weight to the manager at the club, so I got everything for free. The fact that Moses was performing was a definite plus. He was going to pack the club, which was a good look for the club and the owner's pockets. They were going to make a killing off the bar too.

Billboard Live was sure to be packed to capacity that night. Moses was a prince in these streets, but I was ready to make him the king of the rap game.

"Which one of your girls gone be there?"

Fabe had a slick smirk on his face as he waited for my answer. He thought it was crazy the way I juggled Tabitha and Aaliyah so closely. It wasn't though; since I knew how to emotionally and mentally keep women in check. They loved me enough to trust me. When I said don't come to the bar because it's not a good look for my woman, they did just that. When I lied to one, telling her that I was in the studio all night, she believed it, while I was spending the night with the other.

Therefore, they never even knew or suspected anything about the other.

Fabe didn't understand or agree with the depth of my deceit because he was a regular, traditional man that felt like even if a man cheated on his girl, it should be far away from home. I overstepped so many boundaries to him that he just watched me juggle with disgust for the amount of disrespect I had for my women.

"Both of them."

His eyes widened. "*Both*?"

"Hell yea. I'm Daddy. I take care of home. They know to act right. I run this shit."

The pressure to make my words true was crazy. I was barely running my world. At this point, the weight of the world was on my shoulders. I was spending money that I didn't have, trying to take care of the bar and Aaliyah, all while Tabitha worked hard to help out at that house because I had her thinking that money was tight because of slow business at the bar. Moses hadn't even finished high school because I had sold him rap star dreams. He was starting to get antsy, wondering why things weren't happening like I promised they would. I felt things unraveling. I felt my control slipping through my fingers.

I had to make this shit happen. I had to, for me.

JALEESA

"Shit," I hissed through moans that told him how good the dick was. "Yea baby. Right there."

"You like that?"

"Hell yea," I promised.

"Say my name then."

I giggled in response.

When I giggled, he took it as a threat and started to give me dick so deep that I began to moan in sweet agony. "Shit!"

He insisted, with gritted teeth that fought his own orgasm. "Say my name."

"Fuck." I bit my lip, as if that would help me take the dick.

He insisted, "*Say it.*"

Unable to take the threatening strokes, I gave in. "Reese."

Yep, *Reese.*

Not Moses.

I had to do what I had to do. And what I had to do was get the rent money since Moses couldn't come up with his half of it… for the second month in a row. The landlord was on my ass, and since my name was on the lease, I wasn't trying to have an eviction on my record. So I had to call Reese. For years, he had come through in a bind. Before I met Moses, I was messing with Reese. We got along great, he threw me a couple dollars here and there, and we hung out often. I thought we were together. Until I found out that I was only the macaroni and cheese. I was the side. He had Filet Mignon waiting on him at the crib– a whole wife.

    I was hurt. Can't even lie about how hard it was for me to stop fucking with him. But luckily I met Moses. Falling for Moses helped me get over Reese and the wife that had his heart.

    However, since Reese was able and willing to pay care of bills that Moses couldn't, I found myself back in the bed with Reese every now and then.

    "Damn this pussy good," he growled into my ear. He was on top of me with his hands underneath me, cupping my ass. We lay in bed in a Best Western off of the expressway. This was our usual meet up spot. Any other time, I played hard to get, ignoring his requests to spend time with me. I wasn't about to lay up and fuck him anytime he wanted. However, when I needed some help, he took advantage of my vulnerability.

    The only time I fucked him was times like these when I needed the money. I didn't need a nigga on the side to fuck. Though Reese could fuck, Moses handled my pussy professionally. He had that on lock. What I needed was a man to take care of home.

Unfortunately, I had to split the baby. I got one from one man and the other from another.

CHAPTER FOUR

TABITHA

A few days later, on a Friday night, was Moses' birthday party. I really didn't want to be there. I was still in my feelings about the abortion and being fired. Nas wasn't fazed by any of it. For days, he tried to convince me that I didn't need my job or another baby anyway.

It was obvious that he didn't care about what I was going through. He was bopping around the party carrying a bottle of Rosè by the neck and acting as if he was the man. People treated him as such as well. Women knew that he was Moses' manager, so they flocked to him like bees to honey and flies to shit. Men knew the same and praised him, as if he would reach back and take care of them once he and Moses made it big; whenever in an imaginary universe that would happen.

I wasn't moved by any of it. Everyone was having a good time while I just couldn't shake the feeling that I preferred to be at home. I was cute, dressed in a black bandage dress and some knock off Red Bottoms. My hair, which was freshly permed, layered, and curled by one of my girls at

Perfect Touch hair salon, was way more on point than I was feeling.

    At the time, I was following my cousin Jaleesa through the crowd. Nas had selfishly supplied our VIP section with bottles of liquor that he knew we didn't drink. I wondered how the fuck he could afford the party and those bottles, but we "couldn't afford another baby".

    "Aye, aye, aye. Where you goin', babe?" I heard Nas behind me as I felt him grab me around the waist.

    "We're on our way to the bar. That damn waitress is slow, and me and Jaleesa want some Tequila. You know we don't drink dark liquor."

    By this time, Jaleesa had looked back and noticed that I was no longer behind her. She approached me and Nas looking so cute. She had called me earlier that day totally spazzing out because she felt stressed to look fly. Everybody knew that she was Moses' girl. Men and women would be eyeing her, especially the women that wanted Moses, so she had to come up with something while not being able to afford it. She did good though. With a body like hers, she was able to throw on a jumpsuit with slits down the sides and a plunging neckline and look like a video vixen. Her long weave was in barrel curls. They were beginning to fall in soft waves. It was beautiful, just as much as she was.

"Babe, sit down. Chill and enjoy the party. I got you. I'll send the waitress over there to you. That bar is packed."

He was right. Billboard Live was always packed on a Friday night, but the whole hood had come out because it was Moses' birthday.

Me and Jaleesa found our way back to VIP. Within minutes, the waitress was approaching us with a bottle of Don Julio and chasers.

I caught a glimpse of Nas at the bar. Initially, I was only staring because I hated how good he looked that night. I was still irritated with the decision he'd forced on me. Yet I couldn't deny how good his chocolate skin looked in that Versace tee that hugged his toned upper body, jeans that fit maturely and showed off his ass, and jewelry that made him look more expensive than he really was.

As I lustfully watched him, I noticed a fair skinned chick smiling all in his face with a body badder than Jaleesa's. That was the type of shit that I had to get used to over the years of Moses' slowly growing fame. These bitches were willing to throw their pussy at anything, so to throw it at Nas, who in their eyes was the man, was nothing.

Aaliyah

"Baby, who is that chick staring at us?"

With a quick glance, Nas told me, "Oh, that's my whack ass baby mama."

In the past year that I was with Nas, I had never seen Tabitha in person, so I was shocked that she was in the building. Knowing her name, I was able to find her on Facebook and Instagram, but her pages were private, so I only had a slim idea of what she looked like from her profile pictures.

"I didn't know that she was going to be here."

"Shit, I didn't either," Nas fussed. "Stalking ass bitch just showed up like she was invited. Tabitha and Jaleesa are real tight cousins, though, so you know how that go."

"Why is she steady watching you though?"

Tabitha was breaking her neck and literally staring at me and Nas. Since the bitch wanted to look over here, I looked back!

"I done already told you how jealous of you she is and that she don't like you. She still wanna be with me, and she know how much I love you, so she hatin'. Ignore that shit. C'mon."

Nas walked away so fast that he left me while I grabbed my drink off of the bar. I caught a glimpse of Tabitha still watching Nas until he had disappeared into the crowd. I had to fight to keep up with him.

By the time I made it to the VIP section that we were sitting in at the other end of the club, I didn't see him. I figured one of his many henchmen had most likely pulled him to the side. My feet were hurting too bad in the six-inch heels to give a damn about chasing him.

"You look great, Aaliyah."

I didn't have to turn around to know that it was Fabe. He had been literally gazing at me all night. As I sat down, our eyes met. He was standing in front of me holding a bottle of Ciroc by the neck.

I didn't like the way that he looked at me. Moreover, I didn't like the way that I felt when I looked back at him.

With Nas, I always felt like I had to prove myself worthy of being his woman. I constantly felt like I was in competition with an invisible woman that could have him if I didn't live up to his expectations. I was constantly cleaning, cooking, fucking, and sucking to ensure that he was happy. But my mind and heart relaxed when it was in Fabe's presence because he looked at me like being in his presence was just enough.

He sat closely beside me, as he always did. To everyone else, it was just Nas' brother and woman chilling and having conversation. No one knew the burning chemistry between us. No one knew that my pussy was twitching just remembering that hot, steamy night that we had in his truck.

"Stop looking at me like that before someone sees you," I told him, trying desperately to hide the genuine smile threatening to appear across my professionally beat face.

"I can't help it."

Like everyone else in the club, we were forced to lean closely towards one another just to hear each other over the loud sound system bumping the latest ratchet club bangers.

But being so close caused his masculine smell to wash over me, mixing with the unusual calm and protected feeling that I always had when I was next to him.

"You shoulda chose me," he told me. "Every time I see you, I feel like I should have kidnapped you that night. Maybe you would have chosen me."

Along with his masculine smell, the stinging aroma of Ciroc was pouring from him. He was drunk, so drunk that he was saying things that he shouldn't be saying. But he'd been drunk around me on so many occasions, that I'd heard them all before.

They say a drunk mind speaks a sober truth.

"What is it? I don't have enough money for you?" He almost sounded sad, as if he believed that.

"I love your brother, Fabe," I told him.

No matter how my body and heart reacted to Fabe, I was always sure that he knew my dedication was to Nas.

"I love him too, Aaliyah."

"And he loves us."

"Bad men love love too."

My gaze went from lust to confusion. But as I allowed the meaning of his words to sink in, I knew what he was insinuating. Whether he was the wrong man compared to Fabe, I loved Nas. He drove me crazy. He didn't have the perfect body. There wasn't a romantic thing about him. He was rough, hood, and didn't have any education. Yet, I was so in love with Nas. Fabe was a good man with a kind heart that would never leave me wondering. But Fabe's gaze was full of what ifs, when I knew that I had a good life with Nas. The only thing I knew that Fabe definitely could have done for me is fuck me right, and that don't pay the bills.

JALEESA

When I heard the DJ announce that Moses was about to perform, I left the VIP section upstairs and followed the crowd of club goers down the stairs and towards the stage. But as his woman, security allowed me to go into the room off the side of the stage where Moses was preparing for his performance.

I hadn't seen him much at the party. People were constantly talking to him, introducing him to people, and asking to take pictures with him. So I wanted this alone time in the green room to just say hi and ensure that he was enjoying his birthday.

The nigga wracked my nerves to no end, but it was his birthday, so I tried to act accordingly. Memories of selling myself short, to be able to cover the rent that he couldn't, cast a shadow over the day as I attempted to make sure that his birthday was special. I'd gotten my girl to re–twist his locs and style them into a ponytail that was held by bands of his own locs. I'd also styled him for his party, spending my last with a guy that stole boxes of inventory off of a Macy's truck. Moses was draped in YSL from his tee shirt to his shoes.

After knocking on the door, I opened it, not waiting for permission to enter. Lo and behold there were three chicks in the room along with Nas and Moses. One chick in particular was sitting quite snug on the couch next to Moses with her hand comfortably on the inside intimate area of his thigh as he sipped from a bottle of water.

Just like a thot, she looked me up and down, like I was in *her* way.

As soon as Moses looked up long enough to notice me, he jumped to his feet and asked nervously, "What's up, baby?"

I ignored him though, and gave my full attention to the thirsty chicks in washed out jeans, dingy tops, and run over shoes. I didn't have much, but I was sure to make what I had look good; unlike these raggedy chicks.

Immediately I started to shout and point my finger at the door, directing them to where their exit was. "Bitch, get out! All three of you hoes!"

Nas stood in front of me, blocking my path to these snickering, messy chicks like a linebacker. "C'mon, Jaleesa. Don't start no shit. He's about to perform."

"I don't give a fuck! Why the fuck are these hoes in here?! Both of y'all got women in this building and, instead of being with your woman, y'all entertainin' hoes!"

From my peripheral, I could see the chicks creeping out of the door. I also noticed Moses' glassy eyes and slight sway. Drunk or not, this fucked up, haughty smirk that he was giving me was pissing me off.

"You ain't got shit to say?"

He giggled as he replied to me, "Man, you trippin'."

"It's a bitch in here with her hand on your dick, but *I'm* trippin'?!" With each word, I tried to violently come in contact with Moses, but Nas was right there in the middle of us, protecting his precious cargo.

"Give me my keys so I can go home!"

I just wanted to get out of there. To hell with his birthday! I had done everything from slut myself to break the law to take care of us, to take care of *him*, and this was how his broke ass repaid me!

But since I let Moses drive, he had the key ring that held the house and the car keys.

I don't know whether he was saving face in front of Nas or what, but Moses had the nerve to get in my face. "I ain't givin' you shit!"

Again, I attempted to race towards him, but Nas blocked me. "Give me my shit, Moses! Your broke ass don't pay for nothin', so give me my shit!"

"Man, *fuck you*!"

My eyes bucked at Moses' audacity, and anger immediately took over. I aimed to swing, and Nas immediately put me in a bear hug.

The door opened again, interrupting us. A security guard asked them, "We ready?"

Moses walked by me like he didn't give a fuck about the anger and hurt on my face.

"Let me go, Nas!" I aggressively moved my arms to get out of his hold, but Nas let me go anyway. Then he followed the security guard out of the door. The door closed behind them, and I fought angry tears. I sat on the sofa frustrated as I could hear the bass drop of Moses' most popular song, *I'mma Hood Nigga*.

Just hearing his voice come over the speakers made me sick.

♫ I spend money to a T
I wear a pair, I stash a pair
J's drop I get two or three
My niggas got them cannons on 'em
Don't blink when that shit flash
I'mma hood nigga, wit' white money
Fuck bitches and get cash ♫

Everyone was yelling and screaming with excitement. It made me nauseous with regret and rage. Bitches were yelling his name. The crowd rapped along to the song. They knew every word. What they didn't know was that he couldn't afford a pair of Jordan's. He was rocking thousands of dollars worth of clothes but couldn't afford the pot his pissed in.

After his performance, I followed Moses into the dressing room that we'd left Jaleesa in. The three chicks that she had put out were standing near the door waiting, giving us the same lustful looks that encouraged me to invite them in in the first place.

"Give us ten minutes," I told the one with the phattest ass before reaching behind her and squeezing it. That ass was perfectly round and stuck out like a table. I planned to get up in that as soon as I made sure that Jaleesa's ass was gone.

Luckily she was. Moses looked disheartened by that as he closed the door behind us.

"Shit," he cursed. "I fucked up. I know she's pissed."

"C'mon, Moses. It's your birthday man!" I playfully nudged him in his frail arm as I smiled. "You just had a great performance!"

Moses was far from feeling anything that I was saying. He slouched on the couch looking like a man that didn't have fifty women out there willing to do to him what Jaleesa's anger would keep her from doing that night.

"I don't give a fuck about that, man. Jaleesa is right. I'm broke. I can't even take care of her or our son. I've been doing all this rap shit with nothing to show for it. I'm tired of this shit. I need to get a job, man."

He looked at me like I was crazy when I started to laugh at him.

"You're way beyond being a working man, bruh. Did you hear that crowd out there?"

"I don't care about that crowd, man." The bottle of Remy Martin that he had been drinking from was on the coffee table next to the couch. He grabbed it and took a big shot straight from it before he continued with this pity party. "That crowd ain't payin' my bills at the crib. I gotta do something. Shit, I'm about to go back on the block."

I bit my lip, trying my best to hide how annoyed I was. Moses couldn't give up now.

"You can't be on the block, Moses. You're famous now."

"In Chicago! Shit. Not even in Chicago! In the hood! These people out here singing my praises and I ain't even got a dollar, man! My fans got more money than me!"

I sighed as I sat down next to him. As he was about to take another swig from the bottle, I took it from him. "Look, man. Listen. I wanted to tell you this as a birthday present, but you've been so fucking drunk all day that I haven't had the chance to."

Now, I had Moses' full attention. The solemn look was gone and had been replaced with anticipation.

"I've been sending your music to a few people at the labels. Interscope hit me the other day."

Moses nodded, with eyes that insisted that I go on. I almost felt bad for lying to him, but I needed him to focus on music; not working. This music wasn't just his ticket out of the hood; it was mine too. I couldn't let that ticket go just because he let Jaleesa make him feel guilty.

"They wanna meet with you..."

Before I could finish my lie, Moses jumped up in the air. "WHEW! YES! That's what the fuck I'm talking about!"

He even grabbed my hand, stood me up, and embraced me. With that quick lie, I was the man again. I'd saved his birthday and his life, as far as he knew.

"There's no date set yet. He still has to get the execs to listen to your music. But within the next month, we'll be sitting at Interscope signing a contract."

He looked like a kid on Christmas.

Just then, there was a knock at the door. Seconds later, the three eager ladies were walking in.

"Man, fuck Jaleesa," I told him in his ear. "Don't let her make you feel like you ain't the man that you are. When you're riding in a Maserati, she'll be riding your dick. You're about to be a star. Look at these bitches all over you."

As I spoke, the redbone that was initially all over Moses stood in front of him. I guess seeing Jaleesa had only given her more of a reason to get down. She reached out, grabbed Moses dick through his YSL jeans, and licked her lips.

"Your music is off the chain. I love it," she literally purred.

Coolly, Moses smiled and sipped from the Remy bottle. He was a new man. He was no longer worried about Jaleesa or his financial situation.

"Have fun, my nigga," I told him as the shorty started to unzip his pants. "Happy birthday."

JALEESA

I sent Moses so many messages cursing him out. I called him every bitch, broke nigga, and bum in the book as I stood outside of Billboard Live waiting for my sister Tiffany to pick me up. She completely snapped on me for calling her at damn near one in the morning. I was sure that I woke up her husband and six month old that sleeps with her every night, but I needed her. She was my big sister, thirty–one years old, and the only person that I could call since I didn't want to force Tabitha to miss the rest of the party just because of me and my ain't–shit–ass boyfriend.

Tiffany fussed and bitched as she got out of the bed. She was beyond sick of Moses. She thought I should be with a nice, respectable man, like her husband.

Freddie, her husband, was a principal at Whitney Young High School. They lived in a two–story brick home near Billboard Live in Markham, Illinois. He was financially helping my sister to complete her graduate courses at Chicago State. He'd married her three years ago, and had been the picture perfect example of what a loving man was.

Compared to Moses, Freddie was Jesus, so she didn't understand why I continued to stay with Moses through ordeal after ordeal, and drama after drama.

But, within fifteen minutes, she was pulling into the parking lot in her 'push gift.' Her husband had purchased a 2014 Range Rover for her as a gift after she gave birth to his son. It wasn't a Bentley or anything, but to regular chicks like us that were raised in the hood, it was a hell of a gift.

As I climbed in, I sent Moses a few more messages telling him that he better bring my car and my house keys to my sister's house. But, of course, those text messages went unanswered too.

"Jaleesa, I brought your spare key for you," Tiffany told me just as my phone died while I was sending Moses another round of insulting and emasculating terms.

"Whew!" I let out a sigh of relief. "Thank you, girl. I forgot that I gave you my spare. I am so happy. No offense, but I just want to sleep in my own bed."

I lay back, closed my eyes, and tried to calm down as Tiffany drove east through the city towards my apartment in Terror Town.

I didn't even realize that I had fallen asleep. Once we pulled up in front of the old two flat that I lived in, which desperately needed to be renovated, I woke up to the feeling of the engine being turned off.

Tiffany barely looked at me as she said, "I'll see you later. Call me in the morning."

"I'm sorry, sissy," I told her as I reached over and embraced her.

She hugged me back, but it was barely felt. She wasn't feeling me at all at the moment. I'd made her get out of her warm bed and drive me clear across town while I slept the entire way.

I knew she would be pissed at me for a good week.

I hurried into the house. The hawk was coming down viciously. Running up the stairs wearing a thin cropped leather jacket was brutal. The icy December early morning winds were whipping through the many slits of the jumpsuit that I'd shimmied into.

By the time I got into the house, I was emotionally drained and beat from the seemingly gallons of Tequila that I'd consumed that night. Exhausted, I groped through the dark apartment towards my bedroom. As I entered my room, I thanked God that my baby was with my mother, allowing me to sleep in as long as possible the next morning.

I laid across my bed fully clothed with intentions of connecting my phone to the charger that was plugged in next to the bed. But I was unsuccessful. Sleep took over as soon as my body sunk into the black and grey down comforter. I didn't wake up until the rising sun began to shine through the window a mere three hours later.

The heat must have been on eighty degrees because my jumpsuit was sticking to me. I had a severe case of cotton mouth. With a grunt, I rolled off the bed and walked sleepily into the living room on a hunt to turn the thermostat down. My bare feet slid across our carpet quietly.

Moses scared the shit out of me. He was sitting on the couch, with his arms stretched across the back of it, and his head tilted back. I could tell that he was still fully dressed. I imagine how drunk he must have been whenever he came in.

I assumed that he was asleep, until I heard his deep moan that was accompanied by a loud slurping sound. I bolted toward the couch. The closer I got to it, the more I saw over Moses' head. There she was, the bitch from the couch at the party, on her knees with both hands wrapped around the shaft of his dick as her head bobbed up and down, fucking him with her mouth. Her job was wet and sloppy, and I was jealous.

"THE FUCK?!" My jealousy came out in a shriek that scared the shit out of everybody, including me. I didn't know that my voice could get that loud. Moses jumped to his feet. I saw her ratchet ass scrambling to stand up as Moses literally stepped over her to get to me.

"I HATE YOU, BITCH! I HATE YOU! YOU GON' DO THIS SHIT IN MY HOUSE?! WHILE I'M RIGHT IN THE ROOM?!"

Surely, the upstairs neighbors heard my early morning cries. If they didn't, they definitely heard what followed as we all lost it.

"I thought you wasn't home!"

I aimed for his face with an open hand, but he blocked it as I spat. "That's not a fucking excuse!"

"Hell nah. Take me home." The sound of this bitch's voice was like Kryptonite.

"Bitch, do *not* speak!"

The closer I got to her, the more Moses blocked me. That pissed me off even more. All gawd damn night I had been trying to lay hands on a deserving motherfucker, but nobody would let me!

"You brought that bitch here in my car, Moses?!" My voice dropped. I was so hurt. It was that physical kind of hurt that you can actually feel in the pit of your stomach; like a hard ass kick.

The thot was obviously confused. "Your car?"

"Yes, bitch, *my car*! I take care of him! This nigga is my son! I'm the man around this motherfucker! You should be sucking *my* dick instead of his!"

The poor thing didn't even want to fight me. She grabbed her purse and began dialing on her cell as she was walking out.

I snarled at Moses. "You get out too!"

"Man." Moses grunted as that bitch had the nerve to slam the door behind herself. "I ain't goin' nowhere." Then he had the audacity to sit down on the couch in his own wet spot. The sight of his pants still unzipped sent another round of kicks to the pit of my stomach.

"You're shitting me. You're getting the fuck outta here."

"I didn't even fuck that bitch! Unlike you!"

"Excuse me?!"

Moses waved his hand dismissively and leaned back onto the couch comfortably. "I know you fuckin' Reese. The whole hood knows."

That brutal kick to the stomach got worse. I was thrown off, but I couldn't show it. "What the fuck are you talking about? I *use* to fuck with Reese years ago…"

He facetiously cut off my lies. "And you *still* fuckin' with Reese. Folks saw you riding around with him the other day."

I did the first thing that came to mind; *deny, deny, deny, deny.*

"Fuck you, Moses! Don't try to put this shit off on me because your dumb ass brought a bitch to the crib. You should have checked the crib before you decided to get your dick sucked. Hope it was worth it."

On that note, I went into the bedroom, slamming the door behind me.

I couldn't believe that I had been so careless that I allowed myself to be seen with Reese. He and I were always very careful. We met up at designated places and always drove separate cars. I was wondering why Moses' disrespect had been so blatant and bold that night. Now I knew. Though things had gotten bad for us financially, I never wanted him to know about Reese.

Little did I know, Moses having an inkling about Reese and I was about to be the least of my worries.

CHAPTER FIVE

JALEESA

"You bring a chick to my crib and expect me to take you somewhere?!"

By Monday morning, the effects of the weekend were long gone. Moses' celebrity was gone. It had hitched a ride out of here along with his birthday. He was back to being regular and needing me.

As he stood in the doorway of my bedroom, I looked at Moses like he had spit on my mother's grave. "Ask that chick that was sucking your dick to come take you to probation."

Moses and I had avoided one another since I found the broad with his dick in her mouth early Saturday morning. He lingered around the house, tiptoeing around me. I did the same.

"C'mon on, Jaleesa. You know I can't miss probation."

I bit my lip in agony. No matter how much the vision – the vision of the top of that bitch's exposed tracks and nappy assed roots as she sucked my man's dick with dreams of being a rap star wifey in her head– made me sick to my core, Moses was right. If he violated probation, he would be sent to jail. With two strikes against him, he would do time. Despite our present disagreements, I didn't want my anger to be the reason why my child's father was broke *and* locked up. I didn't need the entire hood mad at me for getting their precious "Prince" in trouble.

"Fine," I said through gritted teeth. "I'll drop you off, but I can't pick you up. I have to be at work by noon."

The look of humbleness and appreciation in his eyes couldn't be denied. *That* was the Moses that I loved; the humble one that loved and appreciated me. That was the Moses that pulled on my heart strings and encouraged me to stick by him through this, because he wanted to provide for our family just as much as I wanted him to.

About an hour later, Moses and I were in my truck, marinating in air full of tension. Rich Homie Quan rapped ruggedly over the tension. I saw a lot of regret in Moses' eyes. I knew that the regret stemmed from him wanting to be on the level of Rich Homie Quan. He wanted his music being played in trap houses, in the clubs, and through Beats headphones worn by athletes across the world. I wanted the same for him– *for us.*

"You should let me drop you off at the gig." He spoke slowly, knowing that he was in the dog house and in no position to ask me for anything else. "I got something real important to take care of. Gotta make some money."

"Make some money how?" I barely looked at him as I pulled into a gas station. I wasn't prepared to let my guard down, but if he was able to put himself in position to have money to help me, we were so in the hole that that surpassed what happened that night before... for the moment.

All he told me was, "I gotta make a move real quick."

I reached into my purse as I reluctantly told him, "Okay."

Then I handed him a twenty dollar bill to take to the attendant to put on the pump. When he got out it was as if fresh air had been pumped into the truck. It filled my heart with sadness that our relationship had gotten to this point.

A tap on the window brought me out of my entangled thoughts. I looked up, saw the uniformed cop, and instantly rolled my eyes as I rolled down the window. The police stopped everybody all the time in this hood, but they kept stopping me since I had yet to get my plates renewed.

"Step out of the car, ma'am."

"For what? Look. I know that my plates are expired. I have my license. I'm just trying to get to work."

The cop reached for the door and opened it while saying, "Step out of the car now!"

This was how these pigs treated us in my neighborhood. They didn't have any respect for us. They all treated us like suspects; guilty until proven innocent. So I got my ass out of the car.

"Any drugs in the car?"

I noticed his partner peering into the windows of the truck. I rolled my eyes in the back of my head as the first officer guided me towards the back of the truck.

Cops did random checks like this all the time. Unfortunately, I had given them a reason to stop me, so they had probable cause. Plus I was driving a truck banging Rich Homie Quan. They probably thought I was some hood nigga when they pulled up behind me in the first place.

Neither Moses nor or I smoked weed. Unfortunately with two strikes against him, Moses wasn't dealing drugs anymore; too scared that he would get caught and get that last felony strike. So I wasn't worried about anything as they began to tear my truck up. I knew it was clean.

Or so I thought.

Out of the corner of my eyes, I saw Moses coming out of the gas station. When he did a complete about–face after seeing the cops that should have told me something. But considering his current legal problems, I didn't blame him for being that nervous, so I shrugged it off as the cops checked the truck, but shrugging it off was a complete mistake.

I knew it as soon as I heard the second cop say, "We got something."

The first cop standing next to me, ensuring that I didn't run, looked at me like he knew it. The cat and the damn dog had my tongue. My mouth could have hit the filthy pavement as the second cop appeared at the back of the truck. He was holding one of my son's book bags. It was unzipped and open. Three guns were inside. I was too naive to even know what kind they were. But I did know that there were about six bricks of cocaine surrounding the guns.

I felt faint. I literally fell back against the squad car. The first cop's instincts kicked it. He moved fast, grabbing me by the arms and cuffing me.

"You're under arrest."

Tears fell as I stuttered, not knowing what to say. "But… That's not… Please, no…"

My eyes fell upon the gas station store. A crowd had formed outside of the doors. People from my hood had gathered to watch. I recognized many of them, especially one of them. Moses just stood there, looking on with the most fucked up expression on his face.

He was too much of a coward to admit to the cops that this was his shit.

I was too much of a dumb loyal bitch to point him out.

Aaliyah

I was struggling to get out of the house. With a car seat weighed down with Nasiem, who had seemingly gained five pounds since he'd been home, a baby bag, and my purse, I struggled to get out of the back door without slipping on the ice covered pavement– all while fighting whipping arctic December winds, mind you.

    The sight before me relaxed me for many reasons. I was glad to see Fabe because I desperately needed the two extra hands. Yet he looked so good in a Rock Revival hoodie, fitted cap, jeans, and Timberlands that I hesitated and took in the view for a second, despite the wind causing my eyes to water. He was picture perfection of a good boy with a bad boy image. He was diversity at its finest. He fit into a boardroom or on a street corner.

    "Thank you," I told him as he jogged towards me and took the baby seat from me.

    As we walked towards the garage, he asked, "Where you on your way to?"

    "To see my mama."

Then there was the awkward silence that always surfaced when the topic of my mother came up in conversation.

My mother suffered from Huntington's disease, a form of dementia. The symptoms began in her thirties. The mood swings, depression, and anger eventually became so bad that she was ordered to live in a home. I was sixteen at the time. When she was caught stealing from a convenience store, she was so out of it that she never told the authorities that she had a child at home. I was at home alone for days, wondering where she had wandered off to. My Aunt Sheree then called saying that my mother had contacted her from jail.

Since my mother didn't know who my father was, I was then forced to raise myself. I stayed in our apartment on the South Side until Nas and I bought our home in Beverly. I visited my mother often. However, since having Nasiem, I hadn't been able to.

When my mother was herself, she was a breath of fresh air. She was a beautiful woman, now in her fifties, and was always very smart and schooled me on men. Yet, her bipolar mood swings and severe depression was a motherfucker.

I knew that part of the depression resulted from being locked away from her family. Without around the clock care, however, she was a danger to herself and others. It was my wish to one day be able to afford homecare for her so that she could get out of that home and be with her family.

"You want some company? I came by to see Nas, but I see he isn't here. He isn't answering the phone either."

"He never answers the phone," I chuckled.

We stood there awkwardly. He was waiting on permission to come along. I was trying to figure out if it was a good idea.

The way he longingly looked at me told me that it was a bad idea; a very bad idea. When I asked Nas to come with me, as usual, he claimed to be so busy. He never found much interest in going to the home with me to visit mama.

Because of that, I appreciated the concern in Fabe's eyes and told him, "Yea, you can come with me."

Yet, to keep the distance between us, I talked to my Aunt Sheree on the phone during the twenty minute ride to the home. As usual, she spent the entire time convincing me to relocate to Houston.

"I miss my niece. Now I have a great–nephew. You guys would love it down here. The weather is beautiful. I know you're sick of that snow. It's a great place to raise the baby. Not like that God awful city."

My Aunt Sheree was two years older than mom, but she was cool with me like a big sister. Therefore, I shared a lot of things with her. She relocated to Houston five years ago, when she lost her job at Chicago State and lucked up on a big HR position at the University of Houston. Before I met Nas and enrolled into cosmetology school, she thought I was lost and needed a fresh start. She kept promising me that she could easily hook me up with a job at the university.

"I'm doing okay here, Auntie," I promised her. "I'm on maternity leave right now, but I start back to work and school soon. Plus, I wouldn't want to be away from mom or to take Nasiem away from his daddy."

She sighed, saying, "You're right. Well, wishful thinking."

"I'm here at the home now, Auntie. I'll talk to you later."

"Okay. Tell my sister that I love her and that I will be to see her as soon as the weather breaks up there."

"Will do. Love you. Bye."

Fabe was already out of the car and retrieving Nasiem from the back seat. For a second, I sat in the driver's seat and marinated in the smell that he left behind.

"Whoo shit," I muttered to myself quietly with a deep sigh as my insides quivered. Then, I forced myself to shake off the lustful feeling and climb out of the car. Luckily, it was too cold outside to pay attention to the oddly comfortable feeling of having Fabe with me.

Once inside, the receptionist was happy to see me. "Your mom told me that you had the baby! Let me see!"

Fabe sat the car seat on the counter as the receptionist and a few nurses glanced at Nasiem.

"Ah, he's so cute."

"Look at those ears. He is going to be a chocolate lil' thing."

As they coo'd over him, I noticed my mother's nurse, Brenda, approaching me.

"Hey, Brenda," I said as we hugged. "Is she herself today?"

Peering over at Nasiem with a smile, she told me, "She's doing okay today. I'm glad you brought him by. This will make her happy."

Reluctantly, the nurses dispersed so that I could take Nasiem in to see mama. When Fabe and I appeared in the doorway, as usual, it took her a minute to recognize me. Dementia and failing eyesight caused that from time to time.

"Hey, mama." Yet, when she heard my voice, she smiled at the realization that it was me.

She was an older version of myself. Fair skin, light brown eyes, full lips, a small waist, and hips and butt for days. I caught many old men in the home looking at my mother with longing eyes. Old age didn't stop anything in these homes. The nurses had told me so many stories about catching these old freaks getting it on.

"Hey, baby," she said with a smile as she attempted to stand from the chair she was lounging in by the window. When Fabe rushed to help her, she smiled bashfully like she was sixteen. "Thank you, baby," she told him while giving me curious, googly eyes. She asked me with a smile, "Who is this?"

"This is Nas' brother, Fabe," I simply answered.

"Well, Fabe is fine. Look at you. All tall and chocolate. I like dark meat."

Fabe giggled bashfully.

"Mama, stop that," I warned her.

"Hey, I ain't afraid of no dick. I just don't like small dicks. That's how you got here."

Fabe's mouth dropped open as I gasped. "Mama!"

She giggled. "I'm just playing. Let me see this, baby. I'm going to go wash my hands first. I'll be back."

As she left the room, I hid my embarrassment in my hands. "I'm sorry, Fabe. I would blame it on the dementia, but she has always had a mouth."

Fabe stood with an amused smile on his face. He leaned against the wall with his hands in his pockets staring at me as I unwrapped Nasiem. His swag was so cool that I could barely pay attention to what I was doing. His eyes were burning a hole into the top of my head.

I forced myself to avoid them until I heard him say, "I like you."

I finally met his piercing gaze. Our eyes locked. Once again, my body shivered. "*Like* me?"

"Yea. I *like* you."

Telling him that I liked him too would have only caused trouble. So instead I ignored the urge to do so and asked, "Why?"

"I knew from the moment that I met you that you were different." I could no longer look at him as he spoke. I focused on Nasiem as he lay in my arms sleeping. I picked at invisible lint on his Ralph Lauren onesie just to give myself something to focus on, except Fabe. "You're more than your looks. You want so much out of life. You're ambitious. You're strong. You're loyal. You deserve a good man, even if it's not me."

I allowed my eyes to meet his again. My eyes asked him why he didn't think his brother was a good man. He was loyal enough to his brother not to answer that. It was much like a mother saying the same about her son though; you should listen.

TABITHA

"Eric, stop writing on that cast boy."

He looked at me like I had sucked the only fun out of his bad day. Early Monday morning I got a call from his school. He'd slipped and fell on black ice running into the school and fractured his wrist. I had been in the emergency room with him all morning for most of the day.

Nas showed up, but I was giving him so much attitude that he bounced after the doctor released Eric. I didn't even care because being in his presence wasn't an option for me.

I couldn't even think straight after Moses' birthday party on Friday night. I barely saw Nas while at Moses' party. He was back and forth between entertaining me and entertaining his entourage. After Jaleesa disappeared, I just sat in VIP with cramps drinking my misery away.

There was something about Nas and the light–skinned chick at the bar that fucked with me for the rest of the weekend.

My woman's intuition was on beast mode; that bitch was inside of my stomach punching me over and over again in my gut giving me that feeling that I just couldn't ignore.

I hadn't expressed my concerns to him because I knew that it would be a waste of breath.

He would just deny my assumptions and make me feel stupid for even thinking that he would do such a thing.

I had given Nas another chance after I caught him cheating the first time, but it wasn't going to happen again. Nas walked around like he was the man. Sure enough, he was my man, and I loved him. He was not the man that me and his children needed him to be though. He was constantly giving his attention to the streets and Moses. As his woman, I was loyal enough to his hustle to deal with that. But I was *not* about to deal with bitches too.

After giving Eric his dose of Tylenol to help with the pain, I could no longer ignore that gut feeling. I sat down at the computer and logged into our Sprint account online. After logging in and going under Nas' account number, I pulled up the call details, in order to see which numbers he called frequently.

I recognized most of them, but there were two specific numbers that he called just as much as he called me. That gut feeling now became nausea mixed with regret. I didn't have proof yet, but I knew my man. I knew his pattern. I knew how he courted a woman. Therefore, I knew that, unless his mother or brother had a new number, he was courting whoever was on the other end of this number.

I dialed it anonymously with no hesitation. I figured that the person wouldn't answer since I'd blocked my number. Sure enough, whoever it was didn't answer. However, the voicemail came on saying, "Hello, you've reached Aaliyah. Leave a message."

She sounded pretty, younger, and full of life.

My stomach cringed.

I felt a cramp from the abortion procedure.

My stomach cringed again.

I ended the call, in the middle of leaving a silent voicemail message.

Then I dialed the other number to see where that would lead.

"Kenwood Retirement Home. This is Olivia speaking. How may I help you?"

That gut feeling was still there, still gnawing at my insides like an infection. I had a hunch, so I went with it. "May I speak to Aaliyah, please?"

"Aaliyah isn't in today, ma'am."

I closed my eyes and bit my lip, full of regret.

"When will she return?"

I wasn't sure if I really wanted to talk to her at all. I felt like there was no need to.

I was no fool. I knew what it was. I didn't need further clarification through some heartbreaking conversation with this chick.

"I'm not sure, ma'am. She's been on maternity leave for about three weeks."

I hung up.

CHAPTER SIX

JALEESA

Being in that cell all night was suffocating. I can't front and act like I had never been arrested before. But it was all for petty crimes like driving without a license or disturbing the peace while fighting in the club. Things that I could walk away from after paying a measly fine.

This; this was different. Yet, the threat of what awaited me that morning when I stood before the judge wasn't even on my mind. As I lay on the hard mat on top of the steel shelf, behind my eyelids played constant vivid images of Moses just standing there, watching as my life got taken from me. That hurt me to the core. It gave me a sick feeling that encouraged tears, sweat, and a belly full of anxiety; all of which I had to hold back so that the fat bitch in the cell with me, smelling like her mouth farted, wouldn't take me for a punk and fuck with me all night.

I couldn't even ask God why this was happening to me, because He had given me an out so many times before. After bringing that chick into my house, I shouldn't have in any way felt obligated to do a gawd damn thing for Moses. God had shown me Moses' uncaring and selfish ways over and over again. Instead of listening to God, I stayed. After every fuck up, every ball that he dropped, every time I had to sell my pussy to a nigga with a wife to pay our bills, I stayed. I considered this nigga and our family, when he didn't even think enough of me or his child to do the same. I was so loyal to the point that I ruined my life. I had been this unwavering loyal chick to a nigga who didn't even love me enough to spare me.

When finally given the opportunity to make a phone call I called Tabitha but didn't get an answer. I wasn't about to call my mother. She hated Moses more than Tiffany did. Tiffany and her husband were the only people that I knew with access to the kind of money needed to pay the bail that I hoped I was given the next morning.

I was forced to call her.

"What the hell are you doing in jail, Jaleesa?!"

My eyes rolled into the back of my head as I tried desperately not to let my lips touch the phone. "Tiffany, I only have two minutes. Just listen, please…"

However, there was no listening. She was panicking and cut me off anyway. "Were you driving without a license again?"

"No," I sighed. "Worse than that. Way worse."

"What the fuck?"

"Tiffany, I don't have much time. I'll tell you what happened later. I need you to go pick Trent up from day care by six. I have a bail hearing in the morning. Will you come, please?"

She gasped. "Bail hearing?! Is it that bad?"

I sighed with breath full of shame, pain, and anger. "Yea, sissy. It's that bad."

After smacking her lips, huffing and puffing, she obliged. "I'll be there. Christmas Eve is Wednesday." Then she sighed. "I pray to God they let you out."

"Me too, sissy. I gotta go. See you tomorrow."

I felt so many emotions the next morning. The public defender told me that there was nothing that I could do to keep from being charged with what would be felonies. I was in a car that was in my name. By law, the dope and guns belonged to me. That was that, unless I wanted to appease the police by giving them any names.

Even still, I was that stupid ride–to–the–point–that–I'm–dying type bitch, not mentioning Moses' name, thinking of the two strikes that were already against him. The public defender wasn't stupid though. He saw that I had never been charged with a crime. He saw that I was in school, a mom, and working. He knew that I had been caught up with the wrong man.

"Either you're going to have to come clean about who the drugs and guns really belong to or hope for the best," he told me. "The police don't care about six bricks when it comes to getting someone on a larger scale off of the streets. Cooperating with them by leading them to who is selling drugs of this magnitude would make this all go away. Otherwise, you have to fight this case. And it's going to be a lengthy process. This isn't something that is going to go away in a few weeks. Unless you plead guilty, this can take up to a year. But I don't advise you to plead guilty because you will be facing jail time … at the least, felony probation."

His words hit me like a ton of bricks. Either option was a death sentence. With a felony on my record, I couldn't get a decent job ever again. Going to school would be pointless. They didn't hire felons as nurses.

I felt so many emotions as I stood before the judge. The pain of betrayal swam violently up and down, through my stomach, and around my heart like a rollercoaster. I was delirious from lack of sleep. There was so much anger inside of me that I couldn't even see straight. Hunger pains had me uncomfortably standing before the emotionless judge who charged me with possession of a controlled substance with intent to distribute and possession of a handgun.

Both were Class A felonies.

I was given a fifty-thousand dollar bond. Tiffany was there with the five thousand in cash that it took to get me released.

"What happened, Jaleesa?" Tiffany's face was stern, as I imagined my mother's face would look if I had called her.

I quickly walked out of the county building. I just wanted to get out of there.

Tiffany was on my heels with her constant nagging. "Jaleesa!"

She grabbed me by the elbow, making me stop in my tracks outside of the entrance. Hundreds of people were filing in and out, looking at me and Tiffany like how dare we not be in a hurry.

"Moses had some drugs and guns in my car," I admitted. "The cops pulled me over and searched the truck. I didn't even know it was in there."

Though I left out the fact that Moses was with me and watched me get arrested, Tiffany was still enraged. "When are you going to stop fucking with this nigga?! He doesn't do anything but bring you down! You've been busting your ass to take care of yourself and Trent. Now you have to fight a case! What if you are found guilty, Jaleesa?! You'll never be able to work again!"

"I know, Tiffany! Don't you think I know that?! Don't you think I feel dumb as *fuck*?!" Finally, after nearly twenty-four hours, the tears that I had been successful in holding back came storming out of my eyes. The thought of losing everything was a feeling that I just could not explain. The thought of having to add attorney fees to my current expenses was stomach-churning. "I just want to go home, Tiffany."

Luckily, Tiffany had been able to get my truck out of the pound the night before. Just seeing it as we drove down my block gave me repulsive memories of yesterday's events. I was grateful to Tiffany for literally bailing me out of trouble yet again, but too ashamed to express that as she dropped me off at my apartment and handed me my keys.

"I told Trent that he was with me because you had to work over time."

"Thanks, sissy," I said with a long sigh. I stared aimlessly at my apartment. I just wanted to strip, shower the stench of jail off of me with steaming hot water, and lay down in my bed.

"You want me to pick him up from day care? You look like you need some rest."

I fought tears. They were there because it was a shame that my sister was there for me like that and not the man that I had given my body and heart to for years.

"Thank you," I told her, trying hard not to cry.

She hugged me, telling me softly, "It's going to be okay."

Without a word, I released her, opened the door, and stepped out of the truck. I fought tears and frosty winds as I went into the house. It was a heart wrenching feeling of deja vu from a few nights ago. Except this time, when I wished Friday night that Moses had come home alone, now I didn't want to see his face ever again. Yet, just how life was giving me the flux, he was right on the couch when I walked into the house.

I didn't even have the energy to completely go ham how I wanted to.

As I calmly and simply told him, "Get the fuck out," he rose to his feet. He actually approached me with sympathy and opened arms. I looked at him as if he were a stranger and blocked his touch. "Don't touch me."

"I'm so sorry," is what he told me as if that would fix something.

"Sorry? What is sorry going to do, Moses? I got arrested. You had drugs and guns in my truck. Do you know that they charged me with two felonies?"

His entire body seemed to sink. Once again, I saw the humble and loving Moses that had my heart.

Fuck that, though. That motherfucker only showed up part time.

"What is Trent going to do with two parents with felonies that can't get decent jobs? Huh?! What the fuck am I supposed to do with the hours of nursing school that I have? Huh, Moses?! Who is going to take care of us?!"

He flexed. His chest rose high and mighty as he announced, "Me."

I freaked. With both hands in closed fists, I pushed him in the chest with all of my might. "With what?! You don't have shit!"

He held my hands. There was no need for him to defend himself though. I stopped fighting when I saw tears in his eyes.

"It's going to be okay, I promise."

"I can lose everything," came out as my tears became endless.

"They gone let you off," he tried to convince me. He was so nonchalant about this that it threw me. He ignored my shocked expression, and kept trying to encourage me. "And even if they don't, we're straight. Nas got a hook up with Interscope. They want to meet with me next month. That's why I had to stay back. I can't get arrested. I would have been locked up fa' sho. And I can't miss out on this deal. This is for us. This is for our future."

It sickened me how much he relied on Nas' promises. The naive look in those big brown eyes actually made me pity him. He was lost and willing to follow that nigga into the pits of hell. Unfortunately, by default, I was along for the ride.

Tabitha

"Mama, where are we going?"

Essence looked at me strangely after I suddenly made the right turn, in the opposite direction of our home.

"Don't worry about it, baby," I told her, attempting to keep my eyes on Nas' black GT Mustang.

Initially, I'd exited the Dan Ryan on Eighty-Seventh Street. I was headed home. No matter how cloudy my mind remained, with thoughts and wonders of who this Aaliyah chick was, I was still able to spot Nas' car a mile away.

That morning as usual he'd come home at about two. He tried to get some ass, but I told him that I was still recovering from the abortion and pushed him off of me. His drunken lust asked for head instead. I laughed, turned my back to him and his hard dick, and went to sleep.

I swear to God I would have done anything to just be able to fuck my man and act like nothing was wrong. I couldn't ignore this hunch though. Honestly, I knew that most of the feeling was regret for letting Nas talk me into getting the abortion.

I can't really put my finger on why I wanted that baby after having procedures in the past with no feeling of regret at all. This time, I just felt ready. It was something that I wanted to do. When Nas constantly got his way, I didn't understand why I couldn't get mine for a change. Nas and I had been at this for fourteen years. I couldn't understand why another child wouldn't be ideal for engaged parents.

However, I was about to understand fully.

I stayed a few cars behind Nas, being as careful as I could not to be seen as I followed him south on I-57. He eventually exited on Halsted and continued westbound. The further southwest we traveled, I wondered what the hell he had going on in that neighborhood. Nas had been raised in the hood. He never traveled far out as he grew up. Our home was nice, but it was still deep in the trenches of the South Side. Now we were in Beverly, where white folks lived, jogged in the middle of the street, and played golf.

I figured he must have been meeting Carlos or something. He was the only person we knew who would be in this kind of neighborhood. Still, I pulled over on a block behind him in front of a home lit up like the Macy's Christmas tree downtown. It even had a full nativity scene in the yard.

Essence was too busy in her phone texting whoever to realize that I was snooping on her daddy. Eric was still being pumped full of Tylenol for the pain in his wrist, so drowsiness had him knocked out in the back seat after a full day of last minute Christmas shopping.

    I watched as Nas got out of his Mustang and approached the beautiful home. My heart began to pound violently when he used a key on his key ring to enter the house. I was too dumbfounded to make a move. I fought hard not to react in front of my children. Assumptions ran rampantly in my mind as I tried to come up with a reason why he had a key to this home.

    I didn't need to make any assumptions, however. Facts smacked me in the face as Nas came back outside, now carrying a baby's car seat. There was a thick blue blanket covering what I assumed was a child. What I did not have to assume was who the chick was that followed closely behind him. I quickly recognized her as the light-skinned chick from Moses' party that was with Nas at the bar.

    "Ugh!" I scared Essence as she sat quietly posting on Facebook on her phone.

    She looked at me like I was crazy as I banged my closed fists on the steering wheel.

"Mama, what's wrong?"

"Nothing," I told her, trying to collect myself. "I'm sorry baby."

Still, she looked at me like I was crazy as I started the car.

Mad was the least that I was. I felt violent. Sights of that baby filled my heart with so much rage. I grew sick realizing that this was the reason why I couldn't have my baby.

I was sure of it.

I had been nothing but a good woman to him and a great mother to his children. No, I wasn't the upper echelon of women. I had my faults. Yet, I took care of our household and stood by his side while he fulfilled hood dreams. I was loyal and always had been. I didn't deserve this.

Men are always talking about how they want an intelligent, independent, down ass chick. Then they get one and treat her in ways that only a stupid, needy bitch would accept. That day, he was going to learn that those two types of women didn't come wrapped in a bow.

NAS

"Now her dumb ass don't wanna answer the phone."

I mumbled angrily to myself as I ended the call and hopped in the Mustang. Tabitha's ass had been blowing my phone up all day. Of course, she was calling at a bad time. I was with Aaliyah at Nasiem's first doctor's appointment.

It was cool that she didn't answer, because I didn't feel like being bothered anyway. She had had this fucked up attitude for the past couple of days. Her fucked up attitude coupled with mine was a recipe for another argument.

Everything was coming down on me real heavy. I was feeling stressed as fuck and couldn't figure out what lie I had told to cover up the other.

Moses had been blowing my phone up because of what happened with the run I had him make for Carlos. Moses cried like a bitch on his birthday about making some cash. The moment I hook him up with a way to make some real bread, he fucks up and gets the shit taken by the cops. Now, I was in the hole with Carlos for over a hundred thousand dollars' worth of dope. Moses was also hounding me about that dumbass meeting at Interscope that I made up. Not to mention, by it being the holidays, I was being pulled in so many different directions by the two different families that I had with Aaliyah and Tabitha. They both felt like I should have been obligated to be around just because it was Christmas. I felt obligated to be in the streets doing me.

It wasn't my fault that they chose to have a bunch of babies. They made that choice, and that choice had nothing to do with me.

I thought everything was coming down on me real heavy, but the ton of lies that I had been piling up hit me like a ton of bricks when I made it home. I pulled up in front of the house that Tabitha and I shared. I hopped out the ride. Then I walked up the gangway as usual to enter the house through the back door. Our carpet was white in the living room, so Tabitha never let us use the front door. The gangway was filled with smoke that seemed to be pouring from the back of the crib. It smelled like something was burning, so I ran towards our backyard.

When I got back there, it looked like I had run up on a scene from a movie. Tabitha's face was illuminated by the fire that she stood above as it burned high flames in the barbecue grill on the back porch. Her eyes were red, and tears were streaming down her face.

"Tabitha, what's goin' on?!"

As I jogged up the steps of the back porch, she backed away from me like I was Satan, when *she* was the one that looked possessed.

"Get the fuck away from me!"

I jumped at the sound of her voice. I saw the kids peering out of the back window. I looked into the barbecue grill and noticed my clothes and shoes inside. Small bits of green paper flew in the air around us like fireflies.

"Is that my shit?!" I ran towards her, but the fire was too high. The smoke was thick enough to choke me. She stayed behind the fire. It was protecting her from me, and she knew it.

"WHAT THE FUCK IS WRONG WITH YOU?!"

"No! What the fuck is wrong with *you*, Nas?! Who is she?!"

"Man, you are crazy as fuck!" I shook my head in disbelief as I walked back down the steps to escape the excessive heat of the flames.

"WHO IS SHE?!"

"Who is who?!"

"Aaliyah! That bitch's house you've been at! Is that your baby?!"

Fuck.

All kind of thoughts were flying around in my head, like my money was flying around as it burned in that fucking grill! I wondered how she could possibly know about Aaliyah or the baby. I had been super careful, so I thought.

The quickest thing I could think to say was, "What the fuck are you talking about?"

"The bitch that lives in Beverly! That house I watched you go in and come out of carrying a baby!"

I shrugged it off dismissively. "Girl, that's Carlos' bitch!"

"STOP LYING!!"

Her voice bounced off the houses surrounding use. It flew through the cold wind and smacked me in the face with a hard punch of reality. She was standing on the other side of the fire giving me an icy stare that was way colder than the twenty–degree weather that we were standing in. She was only wearing jeans, a tee shirt, and gym shoes. I imagined that she was so hot with me that she didn't even feel the freezing temperatures.

"I don't know what the fuck you're talking about." She was trippin' for real if she thought I was about to tell her anything. Those tears didn't mean shit to me.

"You're lying, Nas!"

"You didn't even ask me. You just burn my shit up assuming that I did something wrong?"

"I *know* you did."

"You're so fucking dramatic! Stop over reacting!"

She lost the last piece of control that she had left when I said that. Her mouth dropped so low that it damn near fell into the fire. "Dramatic?! You've been cheating on me, cheating on our kids, and I'm the one being dramatic?!"

She looked at me like she was pleading for me to just see what I had done and how I hurt her. She wanted me to be sorry. I could see her heart just reaching out for an apology, for me to acknowledge her hurt. I could see that if I had only done that, it would have made her feel just a little bit better.

I wasn't moved; this was her fault. She needed to stay in her place and mind her own business. Then she wouldn't be in this predicament, and she wouldn't have this hurt look on her face.

"What you think I did is your own imagination! Those tears are your fault!"

She was so shocked at how dismissive I was that she lowered her guard. I took that as opportunity to approach the house, but she soon found her courage again.

"NO! Go back to *her* house!"

I didn't have to put up with this. I could very well have turned around and went to Aaliyah's crib. She would have welcomed me with opened arms and legs, a wet mouth, peace and quiet, and even a plate, if I wanted it. I'd spent every other night away from Tabitha and the kids, lying and blaming my absence on work. But now, just because she wanted me out, I wanted in.

Nobody told me no.

"You can't keep me out of my house."

"You're never here anyway!"

Eric and I caught eyes. Even on the other side of the window pane, I could see his tears.

"Let me go talk to the kids."

Tabitha laughed insanely. She sounded possessed with anger. "Now you wanna talk to the kids? *Now* you wanna be involved? Yo' ass ain't never at home, but now you wanna be here?!"

"Fuck this," I mumbled as I walked towards the steps. I was going to get in that fucking house just to prove to Tabitha that she didn't run shit; *I* did.

Out of nowhere, the grill slammed against the wooden porch. Tabitha had kicked it over. The metal crashed loud against the steps. Clothes, shoes, and burned bills fell against the steps, some of it still on fire.

"MAN, YOU TRIPPIN'!" I jumped back to avoid the flying burning objects. "I'm going in the house to get my shit."

"You ain't got shit in there, homie. It's burnt or bleached, bitch; including that cash I found."

My eyes fell out of my face. I thought she was just burning random cash that I had in drawers, not the robbery money that I moved from Aaliyah's house to here.

Tabitha laughed; watching my misery with a wicked smile on her face.

"Yea, nigga. That money you had stashed in the closet – *gone*."

I was sick and didn't hide it. I felt like she had just set my future on fire and burned it alive because she literally had.

She was so content to see me squirm. It was the first time I'd seen her happy in weeks. I hadn't seen her smile so genuinely in months. It gave her joy to see me crumble.

I walked away disgusted. I actually felt pain. She had turned on me. She had deliberately deceived me with a smile on her face. She'd hurt me on purpose.

Little did she know I was going to get her back for that shit.

I was going to have the last laugh.

CHAPTER SEVEN

TABITHA

I sat on the couch next to my father with tears streaming down my face. He'd come over to drop off the kids' Christmas presents to open the next morning.

Though my parents never married, my father was always an active part of my life. I was definitely a daddy's girl. That was one of the reasons why I took Nas back after he cheated the first time; I wanted to give my kids the same permanent father figure that I had.

My father put his arm around me as I lay my head on his shoulders. Simultaneously, he began to rub mine as he told me, "It's going to be okay."

"I can't believe him. It hurts, Daddy."

I don't know what hurt worse; Aaliyah, her baby, or the baby that I didn't have. He hadn't confirmed anything, but I knew that Nas was cheating on me with that chick and that was his baby.

I felt like I was dying over and over again.

"Tabitha, if he can't stop cheating, let him go."

"I am, Daddy. But it hurts. It hurts *so* bad. I don't understand how he can love me one minute and then be so cold the next. I feel like the past fourteen years have all been a lie. I feel bad for the kids too. I know they like having their father here. I really don't want to raise them by myself either."

"You know what's worse than being a single mother? Staying with a nigga that ain't shit because you don't want to be one."

That stung like a bee sting, but he was right. I didn't even try to argue with him. I so desperately tried to get my head together while Eric and Essence got dressed. We were going to my grandmother's house for our annual Christmas tradition. Every year on Christmas Eve, my grandparents, all of their children, and all of their children met at my grandparents' house to play games and eat dinner together. Then, at midnight, we all went around saying what we were thankful for and exchanged gifts.

"I can't do this by myself, Daddy. I just lost my job. I can't do this alone. Even if I could, I really don't want to."

"It's too many women staying in hurtful relationships because they are afraid of raising kids alone and being alone.

It's okay to be alone, and its okay to be in a relationship," my father told me in a soothing voice. "But it's not okay to be both at the same damn time. The fact that he says 'I love you' doesn't give him permission to put you through shit, and it doesn't mean that you have to stay and deal with it. All love ain't loyal, baby."

There was no denying the harsh reality in every word he said. He was right. Though at this point, I wasn't questioning whether or not I wanted to be with Nas. I was just hurt that it had come to this.

When I heard a knock at the door, dread filled my heart.

My dad saw the anxiety on my face as another round of knocks began, only this time harder.

"I'll get it," my dad told me as he stood from the couch.

We both knew that it was Nas, who had been blowing my phone up all day, threatening me for having the audacity to defy him. I trusted that, with my dad's wide stance and height, Nas would lose all aggression when that door opened.

Yet, to our surprise, there was a woman in a suit standing on the other side of the door. Two police officers accompanied her.

"Hi, sir. My name is Theresa. I'm with the Department of Children and Family Services."

The woman was older and held a stern expression as she and the officers entered without invitation. My father and I looked at one another in confusion as he slowly closed the door behind them.

"May I help you?" I could imagine that I looked a hot mess as I stood to meet the woman and the officers in the middle of the floor.

My head ached more as I realized that they had trampled all over my white carpet with shoes that were wet from the falling snow flurries outside.

When the woman sighed heavily and kept her stern expression, I got worried.

"Ma'am, my name is Shirley Smith. I am a caseworker at DCFS. We've received a report of child abuse in the home. Your children's father, Nasiem Ramli, has filed a complaint."

All breath left my body. "WHAT?!"

My father rushed towards me to assist me as I lost my strength and plopped down on the couch. "What the hell are you talking about? She doesn't abuse her children!"

"Sir, we have to follow up on all complaints, thoroughly," she interrupted my dad dismissively. "Reportedly, one of the children has a broken arm..."

I interrupted her allegation. "That happened in school!"

She ignored my protest. "Where are the children?"

My father's chest heaved. "Why?"

"State law permits an investigative specialist to take temporary protective custody of children without the consent of the person responsible for the child's welfare if there is reason to believe that the children are in immediate danger, and there is no time to file a petition in court. Since its the holidays, there is no time for a petition..."

I had lost it when I heard the word temporary custody.

That meant that they were taking my children.

I was practically pleading, "Don't do this, please. Nas is lying. My kids aren't in danger! Please..."

She couldn't have cared a fuck less about my protest. "We have to temporarily remove the children from the home to investigate this matter."

My father winced in pain. I had never seen him so hurt in my life. "What?! It's Christmas!"

Hurt escaped my face in liquid pain. "I don't beat my children."

"We have to determine that during an investigation since we have evidence that proves otherwise."

"What evidence?!"

Eric and Essence entered the living room with eyes that were wide with curiosity. Regret came over me as the woman and the officers noticed Eric's cast and looked at me suspiciously.

I couldn't wrap my head around why Nas would do this to me. I couldn't figure out why he hated me so much that he would purposely hurt our children like this. His selfishness had no mercy, not even on the kids. The confusion and anger were like poison running through my veins, filling me with a sickening rage.

When those officers began to walk towards my kids, I completely lost my mind. "NO! Don't take my children!"

I was running towards them, fingers arched and ready to claw at these motherfuckers for trying to take my babies. I was sick of my kids being taken from me. It wasn't enough that Nas had taken the last baby that I would probably be able to have. He had to take the living ones from me too. I fucking hated him for that and just wanted to take it out on somebody. I fought to get out of my father's arms as he held me back. The heartache felt like it was going to kill me as I watched my children cry and fight for themselves.

"Mama!" I couldn't bear to hear my children calling for me, especially when I couldn't save them.

"Tabitha, get it together in front of these kids. Do you hear me? Be strong so that they won't be scared." My father whispered into my ear as he held me in a bear hug. Over his voice, I could hear Essence fussing and Eric crying. "Cry when they leave, but for right now, you make it better for them."

I tried to take deep breaths to calm down. He released me slowly just as the officers were guiding Essence and Eric towards the door against their resistance.

"Wait," I begged as I wiped my face free of tears. There was no use. I had stopped sobbing in attempts to show my kids that it was be okay. Yet, my tears still flowed silently from my face. "Just let me talk to them."

I tried to be strong as I wiped my children's faces.

"Essence, I need you to take care of your brother, okay?"

Essence was a lot like her mother. Though she was hurting on the inside, she held back those tears like a big girl. Yet, I sadly watched as two or three were able to escape. I saw that she was pissed more than anything. Her adolescent mind was ready to fight right along with me.

She nodded her head with her lips balled up in anger. Her breathing was sporadic. Yet, she reached for her brother and held his trembling hand. I kissed them both on the cheek and told them that I loved them.

"There will be a court date on the twenty-seventh," the woman told me as they began to walk towards the door.

I couldn't even speak. My father wrapped his arms around me. I buried my cries and whimpers into his chest. I couldn't even bear to watch my children walk out of that house.

I was sick with guilt.

I blamed myself for being so naive that I didn't see that Nas had this in him.

But, little did I know, he wasn't done with me yet.

AALIYAH

Soft music was playing through the Bose speakers on the iPhone dock. Old slow jams were spilling through the house. I was in good spirits. It was Nasiem's first Christmas. Even though he would be way too little to remember it, I would remember my first Christmas with him and Nas as a family. Even Nas seemed to be spending more time at home lately. Last night, he surprisingly came in the house pretty early and stayed in, under me, all night.

Now that he was out buying his kids some last minute Christmas presents, I was putting up our five foot Salem Christmas tree.

Just as I was swaying to some old SWV while adding the purple and gold glass ornaments to the tree, I heard the back door opening. I assumed it was just Nas. Since it was Christmas Eve, I assumed that his friends would be with their families.

I continued to decorate the tree and sway to the soft beat. I was wearing very short shorts and a bra top. My body was bouncing back from the baby. Even though it hadn't been a full six weeks, I was ready for some loving. I missed Nas' penetration like I missed my next breath. Unfortunately, since I was still healing from labor, there wouldn't be any romantic holiday fucking going on.

Still, I wanted to hypnotize him with the sway of my wide hips. I thought maybe this big ol' booty moving rhythmically in itty bitty shorts would entice him to at least some hours of foreplay.

I could hear soft sounds of footsteps on the carpet. Seconds later, hands cuffed my ass.

I smiled, with pleasure, assured that my sexy dancing had worked. Yet, to my surprise, when I turned to give my baby a kiss, it wasn't him.

"Fabe!"

He simply giggled as he backed away.

I said, "Boy, you betta stop," but my body was screaming out to him to touch me again.

I turned around to face the tree and told my body to shut up.

"Put that thing up," he told me in the cutest sultriest croon.

Even though I was caught off guard, my pussy was still just as happy to see that it was Fabe, and not Nas.

I fidgeted with my shorts, attempting to pull them down to cover my butt cheeks. I continued to decorate the tree, ignoring Fabe's presence like it wasn't making me leak from my willing pussy.

I felt him standing closely behind me. "What's going on?"

I tried desperately to ignore his sensual smell and the feeling of his breath against my neck. "You tell me. Nas isn't here."

"I can see that."

"What are you doing here?"

"Dropping off gifts for him, Nasiem, *and you*."

Then he dropped a large bag and pushed it under the tree with his foot. When he traced the small of my back with his finger, I jumped.

"Stop it, Fabe." I turned to him with pleading eyes. I didn't understand what had gotten into him. He hadn't touched me since the day we had sex. "What's gotten into you? Are you drunk?"

But looking in his eyes, I knew that he was sober. When I looked in those eyes, I didn't see a drunk man.

I saw a sincere one.

Usually, he beat around the bush. His flirtation was mild. Lately, it had been the total opposite. That day, he got straight to the point. "Why are you so committed to him?"

"Why shouldn't I be?"

He looked at me like he was disappointed in my loyalty.

"And why don't you have the same loyalty to him? That's your brother."

Again, we locked eyes. There was no denying how I lost my breath. There was no way to hide how my nipples hardened.

To get away from him, I sat on the couch and started to unravel the Christmas lights.

Still, he sat close beside me.

"What did you mean by bad men love love too?"

It had been on my mind since Moses' birthday party. Nas wasn't perfect. He could have used some classes in romance. Yet, I never had a problem out of him when it came to other women. Besides his baby's mother, Tabitha, hating me, other chicks weren't an issue. His side bitch was his work. So, he wasn't a bad man to me.

It was obvious that Fabe felt a certain way about his brother, though. He only let that be obvious around me. I didn't know whether it was genuine or just a way for him to persuade me into giving him some ass.

"Niggas who ain't shit, they know what love is. And they even really think that they love you. But the question isn't whether he thinks he loves you. The question is how much bullshit comes along with his love."

"You think I'm putting up with bullshit?"

"He's not here to put this tree up with you."

"He's hustling."

In response, Fabe just looked at me.

Damn, that look burned a sweet hole in my chest.

"If you know something, just tell me."

"I don't have to spell it out for you," was his response. "You know the type of nigga you got, Aaliyah."

That frustrated me. He was telling me a lot by not telling me anything. He liked me enough to give me subtle clues. Yet, he didn't understand my loyalty to Nas when he had the same loyalty for Nas, loyalty that kept him from just flat out telling me what he knew.

Little did I know, I should have heeded to Fabe's subliminal warnings right then, because time was going to show me just how bad of a man Nas was in ways that were so apparent that I could not ignore them.

And the time would be soon.

NAS

"Cum on this dick."

Felicia loved when I told her that shit. Instantly, her moans became louder and more animated.

"You want me to cum on this dick, Daddy?"

My dick hardened in response to the beautiful shit that she breathed heavily into my ear. I lay on top of her, giving her deep strokes missionary style, trying hard not to bust.

Amongst them all, Felicia had the best, tight, wet pussy. My dick felt like it had died and gone to good pussy heaven every time I slipped it into this bitch.

"Hell yea. Do what Daddy said and cum on this dick."

But the only thing good on her was her pussy. She talked shit and gave me hella grief for being with Tabitha and not her.

"Shit!"

Just the thought of Tabitha made me take my aggression out on Felicia. I dug into her pussy like I was looking for the twenty g's that Tabitha burned up.

"Gawd damn!"

"Damn, this pussy good, girl."

Fuck Tabitha. Crazy ass bitch. She had a lot of nerve. She was disloyal as fuck. She had turned on me in the worst way.

I could bet she regretted that shit now, though.

"Didn't I say cum on this dick? Why you bein' hard headed?"

I felt Felicia's pussy leaking around the thick nine inches that I was penetrating her with.

Felicia had a lot of attitude and a smart mouth. Yet, she had been rocking with me for years. Even after she found out about Tabitha, she kept fucking with me. She was a hot head from the West Side of Chicago. She always cursed me out for not being with her how she wanted me to be. She was always sending me these hateful ass four–page text messages. She filled my voicemail with messages about me not being shit. She was a fucking headache with some good pussy. That's how I started back fucking with her after she pulled that stunt and sent Tabitha that picture.

I couldn't deny how loyal she was to me, though. Though she knew that I had a woman at the crib, she was always there, whenever whatever. She even had a hunch about

Aaliyah, though she had no proof. Yet and still, when I called, she answered. I respected that about her. So, I made sure to come see her on Christmas Eve, give her some dick, and a Michael Kors bag that I picked up from Macy's.

"Shit, this dick is good, baby."

"Cum on it then."

In response, she began to pant in high pitches. Her pussy tightened around my dick. I knew she was cumming. I gave her deep strokes that tapped the back of her walls aggressively.

"*Shiiiit!!*"

"Cum on, baby."

"*Fuuuuuuck!!*"

"I love you, baby," I crooned into her ear to encourage that nut. "Daddy loves you."

I didn't, but it got the job done. I felt that pussy cumming all over me. Her juices were so warm that they encouraged my own orgasm. I hopped out of her pussy just in time to jag the nut out. I rested on one arm with my eyes closed as I began to release. Suddenly, I felt another hand around my dick. Felicia was taking the condom off. She pushed my hand to the side and started to give me head as I nutted. My eyes rolled into the back of my head. My toes curled. I fought to keep a bitch–like moan from escaping my throat.

"*Arrrrrrrrrrrrgggggggggggggggghhhhhhhhhhh!!*"

Felicia giggled as she sucked out every drop.

"Shit!" I fell back on her comforter as I finally finished nutting. I was sweating, couldn't breathe, and was numb from how hard I had just cum. It felt like I couldn't move.

Nevertheless, I had to get up and take care of business.

Felicia mean mugged me as she watched me hop up and start to get dressed. I ignored the way she scowled at me with irritation while I was also ignoring another call from Tabitha. She'd called me more than a hundred times, seemed like. She had sent me just as many text messages.

She was hurt, but she deserved it.

She would learn not to be so fucking disloyal to a nigga like me.

"You're leaving?"

The hairs on the back of my neck stood up as Felicia's attitude seeped through the air.

"Yea. Got some shit to take care of."

Before she could say anything, I smacked her ass and tongued her down. The look on her face told on her. I knew she was creaming between her legs and that whatever attitude she wanted to have was gone.

"I'll be back," I lied.

She was content with that, so I bounced.

I was on my way to holler at Carlos.

Things were getting tight, and Moses was getting antsy. He hadn't even been to the studio since Jaleesa got arrested. We were in the hole with Carlos for the product Moses lost. I was in the hole period. Just the thought of not having the money I went through so much to get, pissed me off as I glided through the South Side of the city. Just the thought of it made me want to smack fire from Tabitha.

I had always been too arrogant to ask, but I needed Carlos to front me some work. I wasn't in the drug game, but Moses was. Since he wanted to work, I was about to put him to work.

I met Carlos at one of his spots on Sixty-Third and King Drive. He was sitting in a Lambo so pretty that it made my dick hard. I was convinced that he could afford to help a man that had been his homeboy since we were knee-high.

Yet, when Carlos literally laughed at my ass when I asked, it took everything in me not to lose my cool.

"You my homeboy, bro. I love you to death."

When he said that, I knew he meant it. Like I said, we had been friends since we were knee–high, growing up together in the Robert Taylor Homes. I whooped many a nigga for teasing him for being so high yellow. His father was Spanish. As kids, we didn't understand that, especially since his father was nowhere around for us to see. We just knew that his mom was black as midnight, but he was the lightest thing in the projects.

Eventually, both of our mothers left the projects. Me and Carlos lost touch here and there. Once we ended up going to the same high school, however, we never lost touch again. We were so close that we lived the same street life. However, Carlos was in the drug game when I was just a petty thief. He started hustling and never stopped. Now here he was making thousands upon thousands a day.

"…But we both know you ain't no drug dealer, fam."

Though I couldn't deny that, I hated that he was right. And I hated that he was smart enough with his cash to be living the life that I wanted.

Swallowing that chunk of humble pie was hard as hell. "I know. I planned on putting Moses to work, though."

Again, he chuckled to the point that it embarrassed me and pissed me off. "Moses just lost three bricks and firepower. Now you want me to front you a brick?"

My nostrils flared with irritation. I had let my guard down and asked for a favor. Now, I felt stupid, but I tried to hide it as I stared out of the passenger side window. "It's all good. I'll have the money in a minute. I was just being impatient," I lied.

"Well, when you get it, seems like you need to be giving it to me anyway, bro. You owe me quite a bit of money."

I smiled to throw him off. "You're right."

CHAPTER EIGHT

TABITHA

Christmas day was a nightmare. I'd been in bed since the kids were taken. My daddy lay next to me and literally cried along with his baby girl, until his wife called, questioning where her husband was on Christmas Eve. I begged him to leave, to be with his family, because I would have given any limb to be with mine.

Since I was the one accused of abusing them, I couldn't even visit the kids until DCFS was able to arrange supervised visits. That was not going to happen until after Christmas. So, on Christmas day, my mother and father took gifts to them and sat with them for as long as they could. My mother called so that I could speak to them. Hearing Eric's sadness and Essence's anger made me feel like the worst mother in the world. For the rest of the day, I was damn near suicidal.

Luckily, yet, unfortunately, Jaleesa felt as fucked up as I did. I was surprised when she showed up at my door with a gallon of tequila and a face full of stress and worry. She'd told me about getting arrested and putting Moses out because of it. Soon after she told me, I got so caught up in Nas and his bullshit that I hadn't had the chance to check on her.

"What are you doing here?" I looked at her curiously as she moped into the house.

"Girl, I've been calling you for days."

"I'm sorry."

"I had to get out of that damn house," she said as she took off her shoes. "I couldn't stand being there alone. And I'm not in the mood to be around my family. I let Trent go to Moses' mother's house for the holidays. Motherfucker tried to use spending time with Trent as an excuse to get back in the house. Nope! Not gone do it."

She was so wrapped up in her own irritation that she didn't notice mine until she looked at me. "What's wrong?"

I sighed, trying to gather myself so that I could even utter the words.

However, before I could muster up the strength to say the words, she asked, "Where are the kids? It's so quiet in here."

I broke down. As I had several times since they were taken, I went into hysterics. I fell to my knees and began to wail into my hands. I could feel Jaleesa hovering over me.

"Oh my God, girl! What happened?"

"They took them," was all that I could say.

"The kids?! Who took them?!"

Jaleesa got down on the floor with me. When I tried to get myself together, I looked into her eyes and saw tears. There was no controlling my own at that point.

When I told her about DCFS coming to my home and taking Eric and Essence because of the false charges by Nas, she didn't even know what to say.

"What?... Why?... Oh my God...."

"All because I put him out...And I burned up his things and his money."

"Why did you put him out, Tabitha? What happened?"

I sat on my butt and began to wipe my tears. It was pointless. I would wipe them away and more would flow to replace them.

"I followed him the other day. He went to some chick's house. He came right back out carrying a car seat. She was behind him. It was the bitch from the party." I bit my lip angrily as just the thought of it pissed me off all over again. "I know that's his baby. I couldn't believe that he put up such a front about not being able to support more kids when he all over the city making them! I came home and lost it. I started packing his shit. I came across a bunch of money. It had to be over twenty grand. That motherfucker told me that I couldn't have my baby because we couldn't afford another mouth to feed. Yet, he got bitches popping out babies all over the city and is hiding money from me."

Jaleesa stared at me with a blank, yet stunned, look on her face. "Did you ask him if the baby was his?"

"He denied it. He denied everything. But I'm not crazy, Jaleesa. I know it. They probably sitting over there right now opening gifts and shit."

Just the thought tore me up. My heart was aching like it never had before. I felt like a man the size of a linebacker was inside of my chest punching my heart over and over again.

This hurt, literally.

"Why would he do that?"

It was a hypothetical question, but I answered her anyway. "Because he's a selfish motherfucker. That's why. After all I've done for him, he hates me that much that he would take my kids from me!"

The devastation lingered in the air as we both sat quietly, in awe, with tears in our eyes.

"Did you ask why he would do this?"

"He won't even answer my calls.

Suddenly, I stood up as fury came over me. Looking at the shock in Jaleesa's face confirmed how fucked up this all really was. A man has a way of making you think that you are the one that's wrong. They have a way of making you think that maybe you are just delusional, overreacting, and making shit up.

But I now had even more confirmation that Nas was the fuck up.

"I'm going over there."

Jaleesa jumped up as well. She followed me into my bedroom. "Going where, Tabitha?"

"To that bitch's house."

Jaleesa didn't ask any questions. Like true family and friend, she was game. "Cool. I'm going with you."

Aaliyah

It was about four in the afternoon on Christmas day. Nas and I had spent the morning getting in some major quality time. Since it was a holiday, his phone was actually silent. It wasn't ringing nonstop with calls from the bar and his boys. I got up early that morning and cooked a big breakfast. Then, we exchanged gifts. I got him a two thousand dollar watch encrusted with diamonds that made him smile all over. I think his dick got harder putting on that watch than it ever had for me. Nas had a love for material things that far surpassed his love for life, so I knew the quality of it would take his breath away.

He gifted me a few things; a Michael Kors bag that I'd been eying in the Michael Kors catalogue, the matching shoes and wallet, a nice chain, and a leather Robbins jacket for when the snow went away. None of it was the romantic proposal by the tree with a three–carat ring that my heart was hoping for, but it would do for the time being.

"Where are you going?"

It threw me off when Nas came into the living room fully dressed. We had been lounging all day and watching movies since opening gifts. Even Nasiem had slept most of the day.

"Gotta go give the kids their gifts and stop by my mom's crib."

I couldn't even hide the disappointment. I knew he had to leave. Because of Tabitha's hate for me, I couldn't go with him.

"Are you going to visit your mom today?"

"I'll have to call to see if she's herself today."

Reluctantly, regret came over me. Thinking about my mom made me so sad. I didn't want that feeling over me on Christmas. Every holiday, I felt so alone.

Nas saw the sadness in my eyes and came towards me as I sat Indian style on the couch. He cupped my face and kissed me softly, taking my tongue and sucking it. Then he growled lustfully. "When can I hit that?"

When he reached behind me and grabbed my ass, I creamed in my panties. "Soon, baby. Just another week or two."

We gave each other flirtatious stares until his phone started to ring. He looked at it and put it back in his pocket.

"That's Tabitha. Let me get over there."

"When will you be back?"

"Soon. Give me two hours."

Honestly, I had gotten spoiled in the few days he'd spent cooped up in the house. I hated to see him go. I reluctantly waved goodbye as he walked towards the door. He blew me a kiss with big suckable lips before leaving out. As the door closed, I melted into the leather of the couch.

I wanted to fuck my man so bad.

Since I was alone, I started flipping through the channels. Just as I had settled on watching reruns of *Orange Is the New Black* on Netflix, there was a knock on the door.

Though I could have sworn I heard Nas pull off, I figured that he'd doubled back because he left something. I hopped up, opened the door without a thought, and hurried away, running away from the thirty-degree weather that was on the other side.

Yet, as I sat back down I noticed two women standing in the doorway.

I jumped back up asking, "Who the fuck are you?!"

But as my eyes settled on the shorter chick, I recognized Tabitha. Opposite from how put together they were at Moses' party, they both looked like they were having a bad day... Hell, a bad *life*. Both of them looked rough; wearing hoodies, gym shoes, and ponytails. Tabitha's face looked weary. The other chick just looked pissed.

They were appalled as I appeared before them in boy shorts that rode high on my hips and ass cheeks, a tank top, and my hair curled to perfection. I was lounging, but I was always sure to look cute for my man.

Instantly, I got irritated as I rushed towards the door.

"You're Aaliyah, right?"

Surprisingly, her demeanor was calmer than I expected. It was the bitch behind her that looked like she was ready for a fight.

"Yes, *Tabitha*. You know who I am. Don't play."

She was shocked at my response. "Excuse me?"

I ignored her failed attempt at being ignorant. "Why are you here?"

"Are you and Nas in a relationship?"

The way she tried to front angered me even more. "You know we are! Tabitha, don't front. We just had a baby. You know this! What? You lonely on Christmas, so you wanted to start some drama?!"

She looked shocked, to say the least. Nas was always telling me how this chick played dumb, and he was so right.

Tabitha appeared dumbfounded as she asked, "Y'all just had a baby?"

"Yes!" This bitch was being ridiculous with this act. She knew what it was.

Tabitha sat there in a daze. I guess she didn't expect me to be so bold. I was pissed that she had the nerve to show up at my house, and on Christmas, for that matter!

Then, her little friend had the audacity to jump in. "Bitch, how the fuck you in a relationship with him when he lives with her? This bitch is lying, Tabitha."

She sounded ridiculous, so I laughed. "They don't live together."

Tabitha's mouth flung open. "Yes, we do!"

I didn't care if she was trying to save face in front of her friend. She wasn't about to use me to do so. "Whatever, Tabitha! He's home every night. He pays the bills here. He lives here! I don't have shit to prove to you. Nas already told me that you don't like me because he left you for me. So don't come over trying to start no shit on Christmas because you're at home by yourself!"

Tabitha folded her arms and smirked. "If that's yo' nigga, where the fuck is he then?"

Admittedly, that realization hit me like a ton of bricks. If Nas was supposed to be with his kids, I wondered why Tabitha was standing in front of me.

"Not with you, bitch," I muttered as I slammed the door.

I wasn't about to give that bitch one up on me, though. I definitely wasn't about to catch pneumonia standing in the doorway arguing with her ass either. However, I definitely started blowing up Nas' phone.

NAS

"See you later, baby."

    Felicia was smiling ear to ear as I stood in the doorway of her bedroom. I'd worn that ass out so bad that she didn't even have the strength to walk me to the door. It was a foolish move to see her two days in a row like that. It was even dumber fucking with her on Christmas. She definitely was going to think that she had rank now. But laying up with Aaliyah's thick ass all day had my dick hard as a rock.

    I had to get that nut off.

    Walking back to the ride, I finally checked my phone. I had only been at Felicia's crib for an hour. However, I had a crazy amount of missed calls. Tabitha had been calling nonstop since I sent DCFS to the crib, so I wasn't moved when I saw how many times she had called.

    Fuck her.

    She deserved to be hurt. She needed to know that I wasn't one to be fucked with.

However, I was caught off guard when I had so many missed calls from Aaliyah. Assuming that something was wrong with Nasiem, I hurried and called her back.

As I cranked the engine, she answered on the first ring.

"Where the fuck have you been?!"

"Whoa! Hold the fuck up…"

"No, Nas! Where have you been?! You weren't with Tabitha, because she showed up at the house."

I damn near ran into the car in front of me. "She what?"

"She showed up at the house, Nas! Talking about how y'all still together. Crazy ass bitch."

"Maaan…" Tabitha was truly tripping. She was completely outside of her body and wildin' the fuck out. She was on my scent. That shit was pissing me off.

"Fuck that! Where have you been?"

"I was at mom's house with the kids."

"I called over there! You're lying, nigga!"

"DON'T WORRY ABOUT WHERE THE FUCK I BEEN?!"

I was so loud that the family sitting in the Nissan Maxima in the next lane heard me through the closed windows. Their eyes were full of concern as they looked at me. The light finally changed. I sped off. I was sick of these chicks acting like they ran shit.

I ran shit.

"Don't worry about what the fuck I'm doin'! Worry about you!"

She was talking shit, but I hung up on her ass. If Tabitha wanted to talk to me, she was definitely about to talk to me now.

"So I gotta show up at your bitch's house for you to call me back?"

Tabitha was definitely ready for a fight when she answered. I was whizzing through the icy streets like a NASCAR driver. I was pissed.

"What the fuck?"

Tabitha wasn't trying to let me get a word in edgewise. "You got my kids taken from me?! All because I caught yo' ass up?!"

"You ain't caught up nobody!"

"You are a liar! I don't believe shit you have to say, Nas. Not nothing!"

"Check this. I let no bitch blow up my spot. And you betta believe that more than you believe in Jesus."

I hung up on her ass too. A disloyal bitch was never worth the air that I breathed.

If she thought what I was putting her through was some shit, she hadn't seen shit yet.

CHAPTER NINE

TABITHA

I cringed when my phone rang. My family had been blowing up my phone with questions about the kids that I couldn't even answer because DCFS offices were closed due to the holidays. I couldn't wait until the twenty–seventh, the next day. That was the court date. I prayed every minute that the judge would see how ridiculous these allegations were and give me back my kids.

When I saw that it was Jay, I answered out of curiosity. Outside of speaking at work, we didn't talk much, unless he was text messaging me party invitations.

"Hey, Jay."

"What's up, lady? How you been?"

I didn't even feel like getting into all that was going on with me, so I lied and changed the subject. "I'm making it. How are you?"

"I'm great. Christmas was good. Why didn't you come to the party at the Shrine?"

"By the time I saw it, it was too late. I was sure that the line was down the street. Nobody has time to stand outside in this cold."

"C'mon now. You know I wouldn't have you standing in line."

I chuckled. Hearing his voice felt normal. It was actually a relief to feel like life was normal– even if it was only for three minutes, even it was a lie.

"What you on today? I know you not doing anything," he said with a giggle.

"Whatever, Jay."

"You know all you do is work and take care of those kids."

A ball of regret surfaced, but I forced myself to swallow it.

"Let's go get something to eat. Let me feed you."

Shockingly it sounded like he was flirting. I was too messed up in the head to even figure it out.

"Your man won't mind, will he?"

"I don't have a man," slipped through my lips with such venom that I was a little embarrassed.

"Really? Then you really need a treat. No job and no man. Your holidays suck."

He actually made me laugh. I sat up in bed. I looked into the mirror that sat on my dresser. It was dark in the room. I had the lights off. But the sun shining through the window helped me see that I looked a hot ass mess. My hair was all over my head. My new growth was angry because I had been carelessly sleeping on my hair for three days straight.

I hadn't washed my ass since the kids left, no lie.

But I was going to kill myself if I had to lay in the house alone for too much longer without the sound of my kids. I never knew how much I would miss hearing them yelling, arguing, calling my name over and over again, and knocking shit over.

"I can be ready in an hour," I told Jay.

"Cool. Text me your address."

An hour and a half later, I was peeking out of the window and directing Jay to my house.

When I saw a silver Audi slowly creep in front of the house, I asked, "Are you in an Audi?"

"Yea, that's me."

Trying not to act impressed, I said, "You're here. I'm on my way out."

Suddenly, I was rethinking the jeans, wife beater, and flat boots that I had put on. Luckily, the camel colored blazer that I wore dressed me up, but I wasn't Audi presentable.

I had already been feeling unattractive. Being with a man for so long makes you second guess yourself. He gets use to your appearance. Time puts on stubborn weight in strange areas. I wasn't the toned teenie bopper that I used to be. I was the color of a Snickers bar. Without make–up, I still looked eighteen. I wished for the high cheek bones and bone structure of a model, but I had a chubby face with big cheeks, even when I was one hundred and fifty pounds in high school.

I was now twenty pounds shy of knocking on two hundred pounds on a 5'5" frame. I could have afforded to lose some weight. I had a small pudgy stomach. I hated it. I wanted the small waist and donkey booty that Jaleesa had. When I put forth effort, with the help of a good girdle, I was still an attractive woman. Yet, I knew that I had things to work on if I wanted to keep Nas' eyes off the hoes in the streets that stayed in the gym and were injected with hips and ass.

However, after the past week, after seeing Aaliyah's beautiful face and video vixen body, I was feeling so unkempt and unattractive.

My current mood didn't give a fuck, though. I grabbed my bag and left out of the house regardless of the insecure feeling.

Jay was standing outside of the car by the time I made it to the curb. When he opened the door for me and allowed me to climb in, he guided me by the small of my back. The smell of the leather in the car reeked of expense.

"This isn't bank money," I told him once he got back in.

He smiled bashfully. "Nah. Promoting parties has been good to me. I'll be quitting the bank after the New Year."

"Good for you," I smiled. My smile was halfhearted, though. There was a bit of jealousy in my smile. I was jealous of his progression in life. I wondered if I focused more on living and less on my man would I actually be someone who could ever afford such things.

"I figured you needed a good meal. I've been thinking about you since you left the bank."

"You have?"

"Yea. I felt bad for you."

"So this is a pity meal?"

"Nah. I'm just use to seeing you every day. I missed you. Wanted to see your face."

Again, I thought I heard flirtation.

"So what happened with your man?"

I looked out of the window to hide my snarl. "The usual. Can't keep his dick in his pants."

"You caught him up?"

"Something like that. I've always had a feeling. But he keeps denying it."

"That's whack."

I chuckled with sarcasm. "Humph. That's an understatement."

"The corniest thing a man can do is make his woman compete with women that she doesn't even know exists."

"You're right. I've been competing with imaginary bitches in my head for years. Guess that's why my intuition finally lead me to the bitch, live and in the flesh."

"Why stay so long if you had a feeling all this time?"

"It's hard, ya' know. Certain men are good at making you feel like your women's intuition is a crazy psycho bitch, that your gut feeling is just PMS. Plus, he was stability. He helped around the house. I needed that more than I needed to know what bitch he was sticking his dick in."

"Don't let the fact that he got shit allow you to neglect the fact that he's not shit."

"Damn." He was so direct with the realness that it made me feel silly. "Did you pick me up to make me feel worse?"

When he smiled, I wanted to swoon. I had always noticed Jay's fit body, adorable smile, and over all sexy charisma. But I had a man, who I never even thought of cheating on, so I just admired his sex appeal from afar. Plus, since he was a party promoter, I assumed that he had a line of chicks waiting to be chosen.

"I'm just keeping it real with you, mama." As he spoke, he reached over and lightly squeezed my thigh.

I sighed. "You're right, though. For the most part, I was considering Eric and Essence."

"I can understand that. A lot of people stay in relationships because of the kids. My parents did it. Shit, they still doin' it. And we're grown."

"See?"

"That's why I haven't had any kids yet. Women are quick to have a man's baby for the same reasons, to get him to be in a relationship that wasn't working in the first place. But a child is a gift from a woman to a man for never leaving, not an excuse to make one stay."

JALEESA

"So you're not going to help me get out of this?"

I stood leaning against the wall in the living room. I looked at Moses dead in the eyes. He avoided mine. His face was full of remorse for me.

That was my answer.

To say that I was hurt was to say the least. But I wasn't shocked at all. He was expecting me to take this charge. Even though he wasn't prepared to do the same for me.

"You expect me to be this ride or die bitch all the time. When do you ever ride for me, though, Moses? I'm slaving. I'm taking care of our son. I stay with you through all your bullshit. Now I gotta take a case? When is it your turn to be ride or die?"

He couldn't even answer that. He sat on the couch with this solemn expression.

Initially, he stopped by to drop Trent off. He convinced me to let him in because he had to use the bathroom. Yet, I knew that he really wanted to be in my face so that he could learn more about my case. I wasn't stupid. He wanted to be sure that I wasn't going to turn him in.

I didn't know anything and wouldn't until my court date. But we were both convinced that the State's Attorney would offer me some sort of deal if I led them to the bigger fish; whoever was supplying that much dope.

"You're not going to jail, Jaleesa."

"It's not about jail! It's about not being able to do shit with my life because I have this on my record. You're cool with being on the block and barely making it. That's not me! Nurses can't get jobs with felony drug charges on their record, Moses! What don't you get about that?"

"So you gon' trick?"

Trick. That was such a bad word in the hood. It was like a white man calling me a nigger. And the fact that he would put that type of pressure on me was heartbreaking.

"I'll get locked up, and for a long time if I get involved in this, Jaleesa."

I blew hot anger. I was boiling with rage, as I nervously ran my fingers through my hair. He was right. If he got involved, he would be locked up for at least ten years. No matter how much he got on my nerves– no matter how stupid he was at times– I didn't want to be the one responsible for putting him in there. Even though, ironically, he was the one responsible for putting me in this predicament.

"I need a lawyer," I winced in agony.

I had until my court date the following week to find a lawyer. That was virtually impossible considering that I couldn't afford one. Moses for damn sure couldn't. Therefore, I would have to request a public defender, who didn't care enough about my case to defend me to the extent that I needed him to.

I looked at Moses, waiting for him to say something. But nothing came out; no solution, no help– just helplessness.

"You have so much to say when you are trying to convince me how you can't get involved. You can't get in trouble paying a lawyer to help me out of this shit."

"I asked Nas…"

I cut him off. That was it. I had *had* it! "Nas! Nas! Nas! I am so sick of Nas being your answer to every fucking thing! Nas convinced you to do this shit, now where is he? Is he trying to help me?! Did he offer to pay my lawyer? NO! You been in Nas' ass for years, and he hasn't done shit for you, but help you fuck up your life. You so loyal to this nigga, when he isn't even loyal to you. His rent gets paid, but yours don't. His kids eat, but yours don't. His woman wasn't in that car, but yours was. You need to try being as loyal to me as you are to him!"

NAS

I had to pick up Moses. So I kissed Felicia, ignored her pout, lied and told her that I would be back, and bounced. She was getting too much time as it was. Her attitude was getting cockier, like she was actually my woman.

If she only knew that she was getting the dick so much because my bitch was tripping. Tabitha lost her position the moment she turned on me and burned my shit up. She was digging a deeper grave for herself with every stunt she pulled. I was shocked at Aaliyah, though. She was usually wrapped around my finger. Now she let Tabitha fill her head with bullshit. She was questioning me, and I didn't like that. I had to show her who ran shit, so I stayed the night with Felicia.

I had bigger things to deal with besides chicks who didn't know how to stay in their lane, though. Me and Moses had a meeting with Carlos. Now that Christmas was over, he wanted to know how we were going to replace the product Moses lost. I had no idea how I was going to get it.

"We gotta rob a nigga," Moses suggested once I picked him up from his mom's crib.

He had been staying there since Jaleesa put him out.

His suggestion didn't sound bad at all. However, there was a lack of dope boys on that level with that type of cash in my arm's reach. I would have to hit up niggas who I didn't know– whose layouts of cribs I had no idea of. That was sloppy, to say the least. Which was why I hit the bank in the first place.

As Moses rambled about what licks we could hit, I actually considered hitting another bank. That wasn't an option either, though. There was still an open felony murder case that I was not trying to bust wide open by doing another robbery.

"Man, we gotta do something." Moses seemed to wince in agony as he spoke. The man was in pain. It was all in his eyes. But it wasn't physical pain. Emotionally, he was a wreck.

"I gotta pay a lawyer to fight Jaleesa's case."

"Man, she don't need no lawyer. Tell her to just plead guilty. They ain't gone do shit but give her probation. That judge ain't crazy. They know that wasn't her shit."

"She can't have no felony probation on her record, man. How is she going to get a decent job?"

"Fuck a job. You're about to be a star."

I wanted badly for those words to be true. I needed them to be true for myself more than anything. Something had to give in the worse way.

I realized what I could make give as we walked into Carlos' crib on the South Side on Jeffery Avenue. It was a low key brick house big enough for a family, but a great bachelor pad for a dude in his late thirties. He had a few kids who he'd purchased a shit load of Christmas presents for. The presents were all over the living room. Expensive motorized cars for his toddler, iPhones for his older kids, True Religion this, Trukfit that, Jordan to Giuseppe, Rock Revival to Robins Jeans. Shit, the labels and electronics had me salivating at the mouth and making me wish that he was *my* daddy. I felt minute and insignificant. I felt like less of a man because I couldn't stunt on myself on the same level.

I didn't like that at all.

"Moses, what's up, superstar!" Carlos even smiled as he shook up with Moses.

I casually took a seat on the leather love seat. It was so big and comfortable that I fought the sleep that had been threatening me since I bust that nut into Felicia's mouth a little while ago.

Carlos motioned for Moses to sit beside him. Though I was nonchalant and unfazed by this, Moses had worry all over his face. I damn near wanted to laugh at this nigga.

With a deep breath, Carlos took a swig from his Corona and gave Moses his full attention.

"Look, Moses, Nas is like a brother to me, which makes you my cousin just as well as his. I know y'all don't have the cash to pay me back right now. A man like me ain't hurtin' over missing a hundred thousand."

He and Moses both snickered at that fact. I smiled in agreement, but my heart burned with jealousy.

"So what I'm gon' do is let you work off as much as you can until you become that big time rapper on the BET awards," he said with a smile. "You bet' not forget about me when you make it big."

Moses' relief came oozing out of him with a smile. His eyes were big, as he and Carlos shook up, as if he couldn't believe how cool Carlos was being about this.

That's how Carlos was, though. He was cool as shit, for a man that sourced every high in the vicinity. To be a man on his level, he was a down ass dude and always understanding. That would eventually be his downfall.

CHAPTER TEN

TABITHA

I was up before the sun that morning. It was my court date with DCFS. I was prepared to fight tooth and nail for my children, and to prove Nas to be the lying deadbeat that he was. If anybody should be kept away from them, it was him. He was the illegitimate father. All he provided them was money. I was the one that catered to them emotionally and spiritually. I was their teacher and confidante.

"It's going to be okay," my father insisted as I rode beside him in his Lincoln.

My mother was sitting behind me, with her hand on my shoulder, consoling me as I looked blankly out of the window and fought tears.

"We'll get them back," I heard my mother promise. Her voice was low, as if she too were fighting back tears.

At that moment, I hated Nas even more. Not only had he unnecessarily and selfishly hurt my children, but to see my parents in pain because of his games hurt my soul. I hated him more than I could have ever imagined I could.

Unbeknownst to me, my hate towards Nas could get greater. And it did as we arrived at the DCFS facility for court. I was geared up and ready to see Nas. He had totally avoided me since all of this happened. I was ready to put hands on him, even if we were in public.

"Tabitha, you have to calm down. You cannot be out here acting a fool in front of these people. It's more important that you get your kids back, not fight with Nas. They definitely won't give them back if they see you being violent."

My mother was right, but my eyes still shot up and down the hall like daggers looking for Nas. I could imagine that I looked like a mad woman. I had had little sleep. Except for the outing with Jay, I had been cooped up in the house in the dark. I barely even combed my hair that morning. I didn't have the strength. The anxiety of being in court had rendered me helpless. I didn't have the strength to do anything that morning. I just wanted my kids back. When my mother saw how disheveled I looked, she sat me down in the living room and brushed my hair back in a ponytail. My father forced me out of the wrinkled black khakis and pink button up shirt. He found a nice sweater dress in my closet and made me change.

I didn't care how I looked. I just wanted my kids. Furthermore, I wanted to lay hands on Nas for even putting me and his children through this. As we stood in the hall and waited, his audacity sickened me. The fact that the kids and I were simple pawns in a game to him made me hate his mother for birthing him, instead of swallowing the selfish, hateful bastard.

He didn't even show up, though. He had turned our world upside down. He had most likely given my children nightmares that would never go away. And he didn't even have the balls to show up. That is when the hate in my heart turned into animosity. I despised his ability to breathe the same air as me. This was all a game to him. I resented that he was still walking this earth. I loathed the fact that I had ever been dumb enough to love such a bitter and hateful man.

For years, Nas and I were a family. We weren't in love, but we raised our children and gave them as solid of a foundation as we could as two parents that loved each other and wanted to do the best for our children. That is what I explained to the judge as he questioned me about the charges brought against me. I cried and begged for my kids. Yet, on the inside, I cried for myself. I was disappointed in myself for being so involved in Nas that I didn't see this in him. I wished that I had so that I could have kept his ways from affecting my children. Cheating on me had nothing to do with the kids. Leaving me home alone endless nights to chase money had nothing to do with the kids. But I allowed my love for the wrong man to prevent me from shielding my kids from his flaws.

And that's what I told the judge as I promised him that I would never hurt them. My eyes were relieved to see Eric and Essence. Watching them as they entered the courtroom gave me back life. However, to see the dismay in their once energetic eyes sent the life right back out of my body. The fear in Eric's immature eyes tore at my heartstrings. I just wanted to run up to him, hold him, and rock him, like he still liked to be. The sadness in his face was totally opposite of the all-out anger in Essence's. She was pissed. I knew that, in her teenage mind, this was all me and Nas' fault, and she hated both of us.

Yet, they spoke to the judge, telling him that I would never lay a hand on them.

Their testimonies, along with the fact that Nas didn't show, were the main reasons why the judge said that I could have them back. Yet, a social worker would do home visits over the next few months to ensure that they were safe.

Nas

Carlos' smile was bright when he opened the door to let Moses and I in.

"What up, fam?" He was super chill when he shook up with us as we stepped into his home.

"Come on in, gentlemen."

Carlos was making himself back comfortable in front of a plate on the coffee table in front of him.

"Damn, homie. You sharin'?"

I was only teasing as I salivated over the spaghetti, fried chicken, greens, cornbread, and other soul food piled on the plate.

Carlos smiled as he stuffed his mouth with a fork full of baked macaroni and cheese. "Man, this is fye! I spent the holidays with Pops, so all I had was tacos, empanadas, and shit. I couldn't wait to get to mom's crib!"

We all laughed. Yet, Moses' laughter was full of nervousness. Carlos and I both saw it as he stood leaning against the wall.

"You'll be okay. Nothing is going to happen to you," Carlos promised him. "That shit with Jaleesa was a coincidence."

Moses nodded his head as if he agreed with Carlos, but I saw in his eyes that he was spooked.

Moses was about to start working off some of his debt by making a run to Indianapolis. There was a customer there waiting for ten bricks of cocaine. Moses was going to make the exchange and bring back the cash.

"Let me grab the bag for you. I can demolish this later."

I watched Carlos' happiness with envy as he left his plate, stood, and disappeared into the back of the house with a bounce in his step that only a rich man with no worries had.

My eyes fell on Moses. He was biting his lip nervously. His dreads fell in his face as his head hung low. Scared that he would be stopped with the dope that he was about to run for Carlos, he couldn't even look at me.

I knew right then that I had made the right decision. I was the only man between the two of us. I had to do what I had to do, even if the only people in the house that knew about it was me.

Carlos saw nothing coming as he bopped back into the living room carrying a large duffle bag. Moses' eyes were still on his feet as I stood to mine. Carlos was busy at the dining room table, unzipping the bag and taking out the bricks. He was about to weigh them to ensure that they were the right amount.

He was focused. Moses was too. So, neither was expecting the two shots from my pistol that suddenly pierced the air. By the time the loud bangs got Moses' attention, Carlos had hit the floor, pulled his piece from his hip, and begun to shoot back. Out of the corner of my eye, I saw Moses fall to the ground. Yet, I continued to shoot. I watched bullets penetrate the expensive fabric of Carlos' black Versace tee. Finally, a shot split his skull. Then I noticed the other that was already lodged in his side. He released his trigger as he lost consciousness and fell face first onto the table.

"Urrrrrrrrrgh! Nas! Shit, I got hit!"

I ignored Moses. I ran by Carlos as he died on the living room table.

I passed the drugs.

That's not what I wanted.

"Nas! What the fuck?! Help me, man!"

I could hear the pain and shock in Moses' voice as it shot towards the back of the house where I was. I fought to block out his yelping so that I could move as fast I could. There had been about six shots fired. Yet, over east in Chicago, that wasn't out of the norm. People heard shots all day and never called the cops. Plus, I was sure that the brick walls of Carlos' home had muffled the gunfire somewhat.

    I didn't want to play around, just in case. I charged into the guest bedroom. It was as if greed had given me super powers. I was able to move the wooden bed with ease. Even in the darkness, I saw where the carpet was outlined. I took it by the corners and ripped it back. Floor board appeared on the other side. Above Moses' pleas for help, I could hear my heart beating outside of my chest.

    Removing the floorboard revealed black garbage bags that I knew contained cash. I didn't know how much. But, considering Carlos' level in the game, I knew that it was more than enough for me. I grabbed the bags and was out of the bedroom within seconds. As I ran back into the living room, I looked at Carlos in disgust, disappointed that he was such a cool dude that he would let me see where his stash was.

    In fear that the bullets would be matched to the ones inside of Moses, I snatched the nine from Carlos' hands. They were already stiff, and that freaked me out. I searched the floor for shell casings and picked up all that I saw. The entire time, Moses called out to me for help.

I finally went to help Moses after sliding the nine into my back pocket. I could tell by the look in Moses' eyes that he was pretty much done with me.

"You gone let me die, nigga?! For some cash, my nigga?!"

I reached for him and helped him stand. He grunted and winced along the way.

"We gotta get out of here. C'mon," I told him as I damn near dragged his weak, frail frame towards the front door.

"Why didn't you tell me what you was about to do?! I don't wanna be in no shit like this, Nas! What the fuck, man?! DAMN!"

"Would you shut the fuck up before somebody hears you?"

As I opened the front door, I saw the falling snow. Moses' hoodie was drenched in blood, most of it spilling from a hole in his stomach. To keep his blood from painting the steps and walkway, I took off my Northface and put it over him.

I looked up and down the block, searching for anyone standing outside. Yet, the snow was so heavy that no one would be out in that for hours.

As I helped Moses down the steps, all I could think of was how sloppy this shit was. I never expected Carlos to be so quick, or to even be strapped for that matter. I couldn't figure out how to get Moses to the emergency room without both of us getting locked up under suspicion. I wracked my brain trying to figure out what to do as Moses sat in the passenger seat of my ride wincing in pain. The coast was clear as I hopped into the driver's side. I looked back at the house, realizing that I'd left it unsecured and the screen door invitingly open. I started the engine and pulled off anyway, hoping that some hypes or lil' block boys would notice the house unsecured and have a fucking free for all; fucking up any evidence that I would have left.

Just as we reached safety, being three miles away and close to the expressway, I noticed that Moses wasn't fussing anymore. I didn't hear his groans or cursing. Reluctantly, I looked over to see him lifeless, with his head against the window.

I pulled over into the next alley. I hopped out as snow flurries became heavy snow fall. As I opened the passenger side door, Moses' body fell out. I caught him, just in time to keep his face from falling into the three inches of snow that had already accumulated on the ground.

Wondering where to lay him, I pulled the rest of his body out of the car.

JALEESA

It was about one in the morning when my phone began to ring. I groaned and regretted that I always slept with my cell in bed next to me. At first, I hit the ignore button, all while keeping my eyes closed.

However, whoever had called, called me right back.

I was thrown off when I saw that it was Nas calling.

He never called me, unless he was looking for Moses.

Since Moses had told me earlier that day that he would be with Nas, I answered immediately, threatening Moses. I wondered if it was him on some late night booty call drunk shit because he knew I wouldn't answer a call this late from his number.

I was still mad at him, of course. We were on speaking terms for the sake of Trent only.

"Hello?"

"Jaleesa Hopkins?" But it wasn't Nas on the other end of the phone. "This is Officer…"

Without having to hear another word, I jolted out of bed. As he continued to introduce himself, I knew that something had to be wrong with Moses.

I knew it.

CHAPTER ELEVEN

TABITHA

It was about three in the morning. I was a bit intoxicated. The bar was dark, so I had to fight to see my phone inside of my purse.

It had been such a long day that when Jay called asking if I wanted to hang out with him, I was happy to do so. I spent most of the day getting the kids back situated and cooking for them. My mother insisted on staying at my house because she wanted to ensure that the kids were okay. However, between my mother's constant nagging and Essence's fucked up attitude, I was more than willing to tag along with Jay as he bar hopped, supporting other promoters that supported him.

Finally finding my phone, I unlocked it, hoping that my mother hadn't called with any issues with Essence. Eric was fine. He was happy to be home. Essence had a serious attitude, though. She wasn't disrespecting me and my mom. She was just fussing, stank, and didn't want to be bothered. I could barely get her to come out of her room. I knew she was mad at me for letting her get taken away, especially during the holidays. Any teenager would be pissed at their mom for that. I didn't know how to explain to her that I had nothing to do with it, despite ridiculously loving her father beyond the expiration date.

I had several missed calls. As I scrolled the call log, I saw that they were all from Jaleesa. I figured that Moses had once again pissed her off. However, as I checked my text messages, I saw that things weren't that simple.

Inside of the dark bar, I squinted my eyes to ensure that I was reading her message correctly.

Jaleesa: I'm at Cook County. It's Moses. Please answer the phone!

Dread and worry rushed through my body so intensely that I damn near fainted. I reached for the bar to hold onto while frantically looking around for Jay.

"You okay?"

Luckily, he had returned from the DJ booth right in the nick of time.

"I gotta go!"

When he saw how I began to panic, so did he. "What's wrong?!"

"I gotta go," was all that I said as I began to walk towards the door.

I didn't even know where I was going. Jay had driven. I realized that when I walked out of the door and he was behind me, guiding me towards the curb by the small of my back, because I was walking aimlessly in the wrong direction.

"The car is over here."

"My cousin. Something happened to her boyfriend, I think," I tried to explain as he unlocked the door.

"You think?"

"She just said that she is at Cook County. Will you take me, please?"

Jay looked at me as if I were ridiculous for asking. "Of course."

He opened the door and helped me inside of the car, even reaching down to push the hem of my knee length Chinese Laundry coat into the car. I was frantically dialing Jaleesa's number over and over again. She wouldn't answer, so I would text her. Despite my anger, I even called Nas.

As usual, he didn't answer.

Jay's hand on my thigh brought me out of my panicked trance. He was pulling off while giving me quick sympathetic glances. "It's going to be okay."

"I just want to know what's going on," I said as I fought the anxiety.

I continued to blow up everyone's phone during the ride to the hospital. The entire way, Jay held my hand, only letting go if he needed it to steer. I had been so wrapped up in my drama that I didn't realize how much he had been there for me over the past few days until right at that moment.

Unfortunately, there was too much drama still going on for me to thank him properly. When he pulled up in front of Cook County, the first face that I saw was Nas'.

I quickly told Jay, "Thank you", and hopped out.

Nas was more focused on the car than me. Jay's windows were tinted, so Nas couldn't see inside. When he finally stopped staring lustfully at the Audi, he noticed me. His admiration turned to anger.

"You didn't see me calling you?! What's going on?! Is Moses okay?!"

This son of a bitch turned his back to me! He didn't even have enough compassion to speak to me during a moment of grief. That hurt. I wondered where his compassion for the mother of his children had gone so quickly. I wondered if it had ever been present. I wondered was I that wrapped up that I didn't see how cruel this man really was.

After what he'd put me through over the past few days, I refused to let him see me sweat. Besides, I knew that his petty ass was just acting like a bitch because he saw me get out of a car that his broke ass couldn't even afford.

"Tabitha!" Luckily, Jaleesa came rushing out of the emergency room doors. It was as if she saw me through the glass and came running.

I threw my arms around her. She was crying and shaking.

I regretted asking. "What happened? Is Moses okay?"

"I don't know yet. He's in surgery."

He wasn't dead, so I let out the breath that I had been holding since Jay and I left the club. As Jaleesa began to explain to me what happened, I noticed Jay walking up. I looked at him curiously. I was sure that he was gone.

Jaleesa noticed him, looked at him curiously, wondering who he was, but kept talking past tears that fell silently from her eyes.

Moses and Nas were at a gas station when some young guys approached Nas' car with guns drawn, attempting a carjacking. When they noticed that it was Moses, the rapper, they definitely got froggish and aggressive. Moses fought back with them as Nas was inside the store paying for gas. He didn't see anything until the shots could be heard inside the store. As he ran out, the kids took off on foot. Moses was inside of the car bleeding from the abdomen. Nas first attempted to drive him to the hospital until he passed out. Then, Nas pulled into a nearby alley and called 9–1–1.

It was a relief to all of us that Moses was alive, but not knowing his condition was stressing Jaleesa out. She just kept saying how sorry she was for being so mean to him and that she just wanted a chance to tell him how much she loved him.

I put my arm around her to console her while Jay stood next to me like a security guard. He was right there. Right behind me. I caught Nas looking towards us. His eyes were filled with rage at my nerve to have this man there with me.

I didn't care. It hurts a man to see another man getting his woman's attention. Yet, it was all fun and games when he was in the streets entertaining these hoes.

JALEESA

I was a nervous wreck. As soon as I got that call, it was like nothing else mattered. The arguing, the struggle, the lies; none of it mattered. I just wanted Moses to live to see another day. I wanted him to recover and be as healthy as he was the last time that I saw him. I wanted him to have another opportunity to be a good father to Trent. I even wanted another chance to tell him that I loved him.

    The emergency room was full of Moses' family, mine, and his friends. There had to be at least thirty people posted all over the place in the small emergency room. The security guards were on high alert, as if terrorists were in the hospital with a bomb. There had to be ten of them making their presence known to the anxious family members and the pissed off block boys that wanted to know who had shot their beloved prince. Even cops had arrived, sitting outside of the emergency room at least three squad cars deep.

    I wished that they would make his friends leave. They were making my anxiety ten times worse. They were doing the most. They were threatening to kill whoever shot Moses. They were crying. I had never seen niggas with jeans sagging under their ass cry with such hysterics.

"Jaleesa, can I talk to you?"

I fought the urge to roll my eyes into the back of my head as Nas motioned for me to follow him. Tabitha was curious. However, she was doing her best to ignore Nas since he was acting out because of Jay's presence. I was shocked myself that she had the balls to sit in that room with Jay under her. Yet, after the shit that she had been through with Nas, I figured it was about time that Tabitha showed him that he wasn't her end all be all.

"I got something for you." Once I was in the furthest corner of the room, Nas reached in his pocket and handed me a wad of cash. "That's about two grand. That should be enough to get you a lawyer to fight that case. I was supposed to give it to Moses' to give to you, but…"

I took it, wondering where Nas' concern had come from. He had always looked out for Moses in little ways – feeding him and keeping a few dollars in his pocket – but never like this. It wasn't enough for the trouble he constantly kept Moses in, though. Moses stayed in the streets running after Nas because he looked up to him. That's how he'd caught his other two charges. Now, he was lying on an operating table with his stomach wide open. It all just wasn't worth it. At the end of the day, Moses had nothing but a rap career that Nas was promising him. Yet, Nas was the only man amongst his camp that was comfortable. I despised him for not thinking about anyone else long enough to make sure that they were comfortable as well.

Nas answered my curiosity with, "I feel bad for you getting locked up. I had set that up for Moses. You weren't supposed to get involved. But luckily it was you and not him."

The audacity of this motherfucker threw me for a nasty loop.

"You know what, Nas? I'm not even about to respond to that right now. It's enough going on. But the next time you set somebody up to take a case, leave me and mine out of it."

I stuffed the wad into my pocket and walked away just as the doctor emerged from behind the double doors marked "Employees Only."

Moses' mother and father met him in the middle of the floor. Many other family members and close friends gathered closely around as everyone else fell so silent that we could finally hear the infomercial playing on the small flat screen on the wall.

When Nas took me by the arm and brought me into the circle so that I could hear the doctor, I cringed. His sympathy and compassion just felt phony as hell to me for some reason.

The first thing the doctor said was, "He's stable." We all let out sighs of relief that could have been heard all the way down the street.

Everyone started to shoot questions at the doctor.

"Is he okay?"

"When can we see him?"

"Is he awake?"

The doctor, who I then realized was actually the surgeon, held his hand up to silence everyone. He was a white younger guy. He didn't look more than thirty and no taller than me. I envied the hand that he was dealt that lead him to stand where he was, instead of where I was.

"He is in critical condition. He suffered multiple shots to the torso. Both ruptured his stomach. We removed the bullets and were able to repair the abdomen successfully. He will be in an induced coma to ensure that he doesn't disrupt recovery. He's being moved to the ICU. Then immediate family will be able to visit. His doctor will be out shortly if you have more questions."

He was not trying to get into too much with these black folks. He exited stage right while I moped back over to my seat, thanking God that Moses was still alive and eagerly awaiting the moment when I could see his face.

AALIYAH

"So you send me a pic of my nigga, but you too scary to answer the phone, bitch?!"

I was livid as I heard the automated system telling me to leave a message. I threw the phone across the room without even ending the call.

"Arrrgh!!"

I was pissed! Moments before, I received a MMS from an unknown number. To my dismay, when I opened it, it was a picture of Nas laying on some chick's bare chest. He was knocked out to the point that he was slobbering. I recognized the shirt that he had on as part of the outfit that he wore on Christmas, when he left to visit his mom and kids.

I had half of a mind to ride up to Cook County and act a fool. Though Nas told me to stay at home because Tabitha was going to be up there with Jaleesa, thus not wanting to cause more tension in the room with my presence, my presence wouldn't have been about Tabitha at all.

I was actually reaching for a pair of jogging pants to throw on when my text message notification went off. I was going up there anyway. Nas could have met me at the damn door. I needed to know who this bitch was immediately. I tossed the jogging pants and dove for my phone. I was hoping that it was whoever this chick was. Unlike other women, I wanted full details of this. I knew men cheated, but Nas had been so far in my ass lately that he had to tell some intricate lies to be somewhere laying up with some chick. Every man that I had had cheated on me. When I got with Nas, I was prepared for the same, especially because of his status in the streets. However, I wasn't prepared to deal with no lies, and he definitely needed to keep his side hoes in check. The bitch should not have had the balls to contact me, period.

Unfortunately, it wasn't her. However, it was Nas telling me that since Moses was out of surgery, he was on his way home. Since Moses was unconscious, he was coming home to shower and change.

Perfect, I thought.

I peered over at Nasiem. He was asleep in our king sized bed. He could barely be seen. He was so tiny amongst the huge down blankets and throw pillows. Looking at Nasiem in that bed calmed me down. I looked around the house and began to think. I had to be real careful about how I approached Nas, because I didn't want to end up on the streets, in the cold, with an infant.

By the time his key was in the door, I had had two glasses of 1800 and a splash of lime juice. The edge was off. Yet, every time I recalled seeing his slob on this heiffa's titty, my skin crawled. It wasn't necessary to have sleepovers with these hoes. Sex plus time equals feelings. That's why the bitch felt comfortable enough to send me that slick ass picture.

I tried to meet Nas at the door. Yet, he was moving so fast that by the time that I made it into the living room, he was disappearing into the bedroom. I sat my glass down on the dining room table as I passed by because I could just see myself throwing it at his head in rage.

The room was dark, so I couldn't see Nas anywhere. Once flipping the light on, I could see him deep inside the small walk–in closet.

He spoke to me, the light coming on announcing my presence. "What's up, baby?"

I sat on the bed, allowing him to finish whatever the hell he was doing. "You tell me."

"Moses is going to be in the hospital for a while. But he's alive. I really thank God for that, ya' know?"

"Right." I barely spoke. I was happy that Moses was alive, but I just could not shake this feeling long enough to respect what he was going through by holding my tongue.

The phone was still on the bed. I reached for it, opened it, and uploaded the pic that was sent to me. Just as I stood to go into the closet, Nas was coming out. I met him in the middle of the floor, ready for a fight.

"Who is this?" I was holding the phone up to his face so close that the reflection of the picture was on his chocolate skin.

Nas squinted his eyes and slapped my wrists so hard that the phone flew out of my hand.

"Ouch!"

"Shut up before you wake the baby."

I ignored that and the pain in my wrist. "Who is that, Nas?"

"Why are you worried about it?"

I could have fainted. Was he serious?

"Why am I worried about it? The fuck do you mean?! You're laying up with some bitch, and that's your response?!"

He simply continued to collect his things for his shower, like what I was saying meant nothing to him.

"Nas, answer me!"

No longer did I care about being put out. Nas was being so disrespectful that my anger didn't allow me to care.

"My cousin in the hospital with bullet holes in his stomach and you worried about some bitch!?"

"Hell yea!"

"Why you give a fuck?! Who living good? Who rockin' Michael Kors and all that three hundred dollar ass hair without paying a dime?! I take care of you because you supposed to be my ride or die bitch. But you standing here worried about a bitch who can't get a dime outta me!"

"And that's supposed to be okay?! That don't make it right, Nas! This bitch is comfortable if she is contacting me. And she real close to you if she was able to get my number."

No response.

Nothing. He continued to collect his shower gel and deodorant from the dresser as if I was not standing behind him saying any damn thing. "I'll ride for you all day, but only if you ridin' for me. I'm riding for you while you're walking all over me! And furthermore, just as hard as I ride for you, I'm going to ride just as hard for my motherfuckin' self. Which means, I'm not condoning this shit! Hell, I'm starting to think Tabitha was right." I chuckled sarcastically. "You probably been fucking with her too. Now, you're cheating on *us*."

He stopped what he was doing right then. He dropped his toiletries on the bed. My reflexes were too slow. Before I knew it, he'd grabbed me by the neck and pulled me down on the bed. Every punch felt like I was being smacked in the body with a bag of ice. I was shocked. Nas had never put his hands on me. He kept saying, "You don't tell me what you gone condone. Fuck, you and Tabitha. *I'm* the man. *I* run shit."

I put my arms over my face, protecting it as he swung on me.

"Stop, Nas! The baby! You're going to hurt the baby,"

That didn't even stop him. He just dragged me from the bed by the neck. My body hit the floor with a thud. His foot landed in my stomach even harder.

I just lay there and cried as he finally stopped.

He didn't check on me. He didn't apologize. He didn't even check on the baby. He grabbed his keys off the dresser, and walked over me like I was a puppy.

Then, he stormed out. "Fuck this shit."

CHAPTER TWELVE

AALIYAH

I must have laid on that floor crying for hours. I was numb with shock. I wasn't a sheltered chick. I had been through some things. I had been through a lot of hurt. But never ever had a man beat me.

I didn't get up until my son began to cry. By now it was four in the morning, and he was hungry. When I stood from the floor, I realized how sore I was in various spots. My thighs and arms were sore to the touch.

I slipped the pacifier into his mouth to soothe him until I could make his bottle. Then, I checked my phone. There were no calls or text messages from Nas. Not that a call or text message would have made me feel better. Nevertheless, the fact that he hadn't at least tried to contact me hurt worse than his blows. It was four in the morning. He wasn't immediate family, so he wouldn't be allowed to stay the night in the hospital with Moses.

He was with a woman; possibly even the one that had contacted me.

My heart sank.

There were two calls from my cousin, Lisa, which I missed only thirty minutes prior. It was alarming considering the time of night and that she barely ever called me.

I returned her call on my way to the kitchen. As I passed the mirror, I caught a glimpse of myself. My neck was bruised and purple in color. That made anger burn on the inside of my heart. I left the mirror realizing that this nigga had really put his hands on me; all because I asked him why he was disloyal.

"Hello?"

I was completely caught off guard when Lisa answered the phone with the same tears in her voice that I had in my eyes. It was so quiet in her background that I could hear the engine of her car and the tires as they hit different bumps in the road.

"Lisa, what's wrong?"

Instantly, my heart filled with fear. For her to call me, it had to be something bad. I was sure that this had to be bad news regarding one of our family members.

Yet, I was wrong.

"Have you heard? Did Nas tell you?"

"Tell me what?"

When she mentioned Nas' name, I instantly assumed that Moses hadn't made it.

However, it was worse– way worse.

Sobs overshadowed her words. It was hard for her to speak, but I could still make out what she said. "They killed him. Somebody killed Carlos."

My heart sank for her. Unfortunately, when dealing with men that lived in the streets, in the back of your mind, you expect this. You pray against it every day, but that was the world we lived in. Yet, I knew that having the preconceived notion didn't make it any better. It still hurt. That hurt poured through the phone. I stopped my tears in order to comfort hers.

"I'm so sorry, Lisa. When?"

She told me that nobody was sure. Carlos' mother had only called a few hours ago, telling her that Renee, the mother of Carlos' younger children, had called when she found him in the house, dead with gunshots wounds in the head and side. She'd forced her way inside when she'd gone over to his house to check on him, saw his car outside, but wasn't getting an answer when she called or rang the doorbell. In the short time since, news spread through the streets that Renee had also said that she immediately went to his stash, since she knew where it was, to clean it out before the cops came. Cops were good for stealing most cash and only submitting a small portion of it as evidence.

Carlos' stash was completely empty of cash.

"Somebody got him, but whoever it is gon' get caught easy, if they stay in Chicago. He had to have over three hundred thousand dollars stashed away. Dumb niggas will start flossing for sure."

Her words were filled with so much rage. Even though she and Carlos hadn't been together for years, they had a great relationship. He took very good care of her and her children.

"I'm on my way to Chicago. I'm only about thirty minutes away now."

"Okay," I told her. "I'll see you in a minute."

"Girl, don't bring that baby out in this weather. It's snowing like crazy. The roads are horrible. If I need you, I'll call you."

I wanted to be there for her, but honestly I was relieved as I hung up the phone. She was experiencing physical death. She had closer friends and cousins to help her cope, though. However, I was experiencing an emotional death and didn't have anyone to help me deal.

My baby lay on the bed, looking at me with the most beautiful dough eyes. I watched him, wanting to be sure that I gave him the best mother and father figure that I could. A man that would put his hands on his woman was not what I wanted as a father figure for Nasiem. A woman that would put up with that was not what I wanted to portray as a mother.

If the cheating and abuse wasn't a sure sign to leave, that was. Being stupid enough to allow Nas to affect my life was one thing, but my child's life was off limits.

I went to the closet to pack, hoping that the pacifier would soothe Nasiem long enough to allow me to do so.

As I packed, I figured that I had no choice but to finally take Aunt Sheree up on her offer to move to Houston. I didn't have enough of my own money to make the drive, so after packing, I left the bedroom to dip in Nas' stash.

It was the least he owed me.

While I entered the living room and moved the couch, I prayed that Nas wouldn't return and catch me. Nas had been in such a rush the last time that he was there that he hadn't even secured the floorboards. Dusty garbage bags stuck out. To my surprise, there was way more than the usual ten or so thousand inside. Lo and behold, I opened the bags to lay my eyes on bundles and bundles of cash. It was more money than I had ever seen before.

I sat on the floor in a daze, shocked at the countless faces of dead presidents looking back at me. I couldn't even guess how much money it was.

I wondered where the hell Nas would get this kind of money. Weight had to be sold to make this kind of money, and a lot of it. Nas wasn't on that level, no matter how bad he wanted to be. We didn't even know people with this kind of paper.

Then, it dawned on me. I gasped so loud that my astonishment echoed through the house.

It wasn't a coincidence; Carlos, his empty stash, and this cash. It all made sense.

The realization made me nauseous. The depths of Nas' greed and deceit made me sick with anger. I couldn't imagine the kind of man that I had given my life to.

Yet, what I *could* imagine was that it was enough money to take care of myself, my mother, and my son for a very long time.

JALEESA

The last thing I wanted to do was sit in a court room. I couldn't miss the preliminary hearing. So, I didn't have a choice. I would have much rather been at the hospital waiting for them to wake up Moses. If I had missed court though, they would put a warrant out for my arrest. Reluctantly, I left Moses' bedside. He was still out, but I wanted to be the first face that he saw when they woke him up.

There was such an eerie feeling over me. I didn't understand what was happening to me and my family. They say that you go through the worst storm right before your blessing. Yet, my vision was blurry. I couldn't tell whether this was a blessing on its way or hell that I put myself in because of my bad decisions.

"How much time can I get if I just plead guilty?"

The public defender assigned to my case looked at me like I was crazy. He was a white older man. Therefore, his face flushed red as he thought about it.

"Are you sure that you want to do that?"

I looked into those ocean blue eyes and nodded my head.

I know that I was giving up. Yet, after seeing Moses lay in that bed appearing lifeless, I realized what was really important in life. Above my job at Target, even above nursing school, my family was the most important thing to me. Moses wasn't perfect. However, if his only problem was making money, then with the love of his family, we could fix that. He hadn't set me up. Nas told me how bad Moses wanted to get some money to make it better between him and I. He was so desperate that he was willing to make that run knowing what was at risk. It was unfortunate how things had played out. Yet, when I weighed possible probation against putting the father of my child in jail for the rest of his life, I just couldn't do it.

It wasn't an option.

"Yes," I finally answered. Even though in my heart I felt like what I was doing was right, I prayed to God that I was doing the right thing; that it wouldn't come back and smack me in the face with a dose of regret.

"How much time can I get?"

"You don't have a record. The least you can get is probation."

"And the most that I can get?"

"Five or six years. You would have to do at least half that time."

I leaned against the wall of the hallway. The public defender and I were standing in the hallway waiting for court to start. I was hiding my face behind the black scarf wrapped around my neck to hide from the cold in the old building. I was also hiding from the potential of my life being over because, even after everything that had happened, I was being more loyal to a man than he was to me.

All I could think about was Moses, though. Everything had my mind completely gone. I didn't care about these charges. Of course, I would have liked Moses to be a hero and save the day. I would have liked for him to be willing to sacrifice himself, own up to the drugs and guns, and free me of this. It wasn't that easy, though. With two strikes already against him, he would have been sent away forever. When I thought rationally, probation, or even a few years, was nothing compared to him never coming home, never seeing my child again.

I just wanted it to go away. I just wanted Moses to be okay.

TABITHA

After Jaleesa's court date, I met her up at the hospital. The crowd that was once in the emergency room during the early hours of the morning had now relocated to the waiting area of the ICU. I couldn't even count how many times these niggas got into it with security. They didn't care about the capacity limit. They didn't care about keeping it down because of the patients either.

    It was a mad house. Things were even worse because word had hit the streets that Carlos was found dead in his home. Nobody had any full details, but I assumed that it was a robbery. Everyone had gone from worried about Moses to distraught over Carlos. No matter the work he was in, Carlos was a cool dude. He was good to the guys that worked for him, gave back to the hood, and never condoned killing anyone, no matter if they owed him money or threatened his life.

    Despite the shit that he had put me through, my heart still went out to Nas, as I watched him sick in a corner, torn after hearing the news that his best friend was dead. I felt terrible and wished that things were different so that I felt comfortable enough to console him.

But fuck that. I recalled countless times over the past weeks that I was just as torn, and nothing in him moved him to console me.

"So what happened at court?"

Jaleesa and I were in the hallway, staring out of the picture windows as snow fell on the city. I was so sick of seeing snow that I didn't know what to do with myself. It had to be at least eight inches of snow already, and it was still falling.

"It was just a preliminary hearing. They assigned the case to a judge. We were hoping it would be thrown out, but it wasn't."

I didn't attempt to hide how disappointed I was. This shit was foul. Jaleesa didn't deserve this. She was a good mother and had always been a good woman to Moses. She literally carried that family on her back while he chased this rap dream with Nas.

This was the thanks she got.

I felt personally responsible. Not only did my man set it up, but I was the one that introduced her to Moses in the first place.

"I can get up to five years. My lawyer thinks that I will most likely get felony probation since I don't have a record."

"That's still fucked up."

"I know."

"You have to wait seven years to get a felony off of your record, and it costs a lot."

"I know," she repeated with a sigh. "It's obvious that the drugs weren't mine. But they want me to trick on whose they really were. I just can't do it. I don't care how much Moses gets on my nerves; I can't put Moses in the middle of this. They'll lock him up without thinking twice. I can't have that on my conscience."

I use to wonder how chicks found themselves locked up because of their man. Now, I knew. I couldn't imagine having to make that choice, *in the past*. It was like literally choosing between snitching on your family or sacrificing yourself.

"Since Nas gave me some money to get a real lawyer, maybe I can find a good one that can just win the case."

My eyes squinted with curiosity. "How much did he give you?"

"Two thousand to hire a good lawyer. He said he would pay the rest as the case went on. So, that's good."

Of course, I was super curious about where this sudden compassion in Nas came from. He had been a complete ass to me and his children, but felt the need to pay Jaleesa's lawyer. I was happy that she now had the money to hire someone to help her fight this. However, the realization that Nas cared more about her case than he did about me, or even his kids, made my hate for him grow like a wild weed.

Seeing the disgust that darted out of my eyes, Jaleesa asked, "Have you all talked?"

My eyes rolled into the back of my head. "No. He has the nerve to be mad at me. Ain't that a bitch?"

"He is really acting a fool. Why is he so upset?"

"I turned on him, is what he keeps saying. Can you believe that? He steps out on me, has a baby on me, but I turned on him? *I'm* the disloyal one? He's full of himself. He doesn't see the error in his ways. He never does. He's always right, and I'm always just trippin'."

Just talking about it raised the level of anger that had been sitting with me since this all began. Nas had a lot of nerve. I hated even being in that hospital because he was there. I hated being in the same room with his ass.

All he had to do was tell me. Had he told me that he had a chick on the side pregnant, I would have told him to step and still had my baby. Both of us could have gotten what we wanted. But no, Nas was too selfish and vain to think enough about me to do such a thing. He wanted his cake, to eat it too, the pie, and the motherfucking filling.

What turned my face red with rage was the fact that that bitch could have her baby, but I couldn't. I had been with him for over ten years. I had given him so much of me; my youth, my children. And some bitch that just comes along can get the nice house and family that I couldn't convince this nigga to give me.

"How are the kids doing now that they are back home?"

"Eric is fine. He's just happy to be home. But with Essence, something isn't right. She's just pissed off. She's snapping on everybody. Getting into screaming matches with Eric. It's not like her."

"Well, being snatched out of your home is a lot to deal with. And she is a teenager. She's probably just mad she missed Christmas."

"I can't believe Nas was that mad at me. All because I left him? Because I burned up a couple grand? My children equate to a couple thousand dollars? That nigga is so twisted." My mouth balled up as I fought the stinging in my eyes that was introducing tears.

I was so sick of crying.

"Tabitha, it's going to be okay," Jaleesa said as she wiped my face. As she did so, I noticed three guys getting off of the elevator. One of them was so familiar to me, but I couldn't place him. I guess I was familiar to him too, since he did a double take when he saw me.

"Who are they? Friends of Moses?"

Jaleesa took a quick glance and then turned back to me. "Probably. I've never seen them before. There have been so many people coming in and out of here, girl. But you know who hasn't shown up?"

"Who?"

"A chick."

"What chick?"

She shrugged her shoulders. "Hell, any chick. I never trusted Moses. I always thought he was cheating, even though the first time I caught him was the night of his birthday party. But not one woman has come to visit him, not even a friend. I swore he was lying about being in the studio all of those nights, but I guess I was wrong. He really was working. He wants to be successful so bad."

So much grief came over her at that moment. I wrapped my arms around her. She buried her face in my shoulder as I buried mine in hers. In such a short time, our worlds had been turned upside down. It was a lot to take in, and it was hard as hell to be strong.

"I just want him to be okay."

I matched Jaleesa's somber tone as I told her, "He will."

"I treated him so bad. All because he was struggling. That wasn't right. I just want to tell him that I'm sorry.

"You'll get the chance to."

"I hope so," she admitted with dread. "I really *really* hope so."

Nas

"Let me holla at you outside, man."

I wasn't comfortable leaving the waiting area. I had been lingering around like a fruit fly since everything went down. I had to be sure that I was there when Moses woke up. He needed to know what story to tell the police so that our stories would match.

If we stuck to our story, there would be no way that we could be linked to Carlos' murder.

I wasn't sure if Moses would still fuck with me like he used to once he woke up. Though there was a lot of pain in his eyes before they closed, I could also see there was a lot of disappointment in me.

Nothing in me felt bad for how I played this, though. Had I told Moses what I was planning that night, Moses would have chickened out and I would have missed my opportunity. I took a big gamble with his life. Yet, the guap that I obtained in the process was well worth it. I planned to give Moses a nice portion of it so that he would feel the same.

I had to sit on the money for a minute until Carlos' death settled down on the street. I needed to figure out a way to introduce this new wealth without looking suspect. Yet and still, the world was my oyster now. I could do anything that I had been obsessing about in my mind. Anything I wanted was now in the palms of my hands. I could be the man that I wanted to be.

I'd done it all by myself. That's what I thought as I made small talk with Caine as we took the elevator to the lobby. I didn't need these helpless niggas no more. They did nothing to assist in getting me to the next level, though I was the reason why they were able to eat.

This was their last stop, including Tabitha, Aaliyah, and Felicia's big mouth ass. I was letting their dead weight off so that I could take this new ride to wealth solo.

"So what's up? Why you call me out here in this shit? It's cold as fuck." I hid my face behind the collar of my Moncler coat and stuffed my hands in my pockets as Caine looked at me nervously. "Speak, nigga."

"I think your girl recognized me," he told me. "She looked at me like she knew me from somewhere."

"Your faces were covered, though."

"I know. I'm just telling you what I saw. She did a double take and started talking to the chick that she was with. She had tears in her eyes like she was spooked."

Fuck.

If she recognized Caine, it was only from the robbery. Days after I met him, I began to put the plan in motion to rob the bank. I knew that I was going to use him to do it, so I kept him and Lavell away from Tabitha so that she wouldn't suspect anything when they hit the bank.

I didn't need this shit. Tabitha had been on a running–her–mouth spree. She was not about to fuck this money up for me like she did the last.

"Get rid of her," came smoothly out of my mouth with no hesitation.

Caine squinted his eyes and cocked his head slowly, as if that would assist in helping him understanding me more clearly. "Get rid of her?"

"Yes, nigga. I'm not taking no chances. You shouldn't either."

He told me, "That's your kids' mother," as if that would put some type of compassion in my heart. I didn't give a fuck. She was also a bitch that had turned on me, a bitch that was willing to do anything to hurt me, a bitch that had been doing anything to fuck up shit for me.

"Don't facing life sound serious?"

Caine looked disgusted and shocked, like he'd swallowed his own shit. Before he could find the words to say, I waved my hand dismissively. I turned away, disgusted that he was being so scary.

Fuck it, I thought. *I'll do it myself.*

CHAPTER THIRTEEN

NAS

I hadn't heard from Aaliyah since the morning before, when I left her ass on the floor. That was fine by me. All of these hoes were getting out of pocket. They could all kiss my ass. I had something special for Tabitha's snitching ass, though. I had no mercy for her. She was about to kiss the ground six feet deep.

I needed to shower, change, and get my shit out Aaliyah's crib, though. The house was in Aaliyah's name, so she could figure out how to keep up with the mortgage for all I gave a fuck about. I had enough bread to get my own shit now.

I knew it would be some beef with her as soon as I walked through the door, so I prepared myself for it. What I wasn't prepared for was the empty house that I walked into.

It was too early in the morning for Aaliyah to be outside, especially with the baby. I walked into the bedroom and noticed that everything was still on the floor from our fight. Since she hadn't attempted to even pick up anything, I knew that she had split.

It was fine by me. That house could have gone up in flames. It was her problem. Not mine.

It did, however, become a problem for me when I went into the stash to grab some cash and noticed that the garbage bags were gone.

"SHIT!"

Aaliyah had to have taken them.

I punched the walls over and over again, until drywall collapsed around my hands and my knuckles bled.

"Fuck, man!"

I heard the back door open. I hadn't locked it behind myself. I hoped that it was Aaliyah. I walked towards the kitchen, where the back door was. I was prepared to stump a hole in this bitch.

Unfortunately, it was Fabe who emerged from the kitchen.

"What's wrong with you?" Fabe looked at me like I was crazy as I stood in the middle of the living room floor with my fists balled up, flared nostrils, and bleeding knuckles.

"You seen Aaliyah?"

"Nah."

I immediately took my cell from my pocket. I dialed her number as Fabe followed me into the living room and took a seat on the couch.

My call went straight to voicemail.

I called again.

And again.

And again.

Each time, it went straight to voicemail.

"FUCK!"

Fabe jumped at the sound of my voice as I fought the urge to throw the phone across the room.

"What the hell is wrong with you, fam?"

I exhaled long and slow as I tried to keep myself from freaking out. Since Aaliyah had the cash, once she heard about Carlos' murder, she would put two and two together. Since she had the balls to take it, she didn't plan on letting me find her. I knew it.

"Aaliyah's gone."

My brother's mouth dropped. He looked just as thrown off as I did.

"Why she leave?"

"I hit her."

Instantly, Fabe's face changed from confused to pissed, which shocked the fuck outta me. I'd hit my girl, not his.

"What the fuck is wrong with you, man?" He was actually waiting for an answer to that question, sitting on the couch, looking at me like he was disappointed in me.

"Man, she was trippin'! All in my face because Felicia's dumb ass sent her a picture of me in her bed sleep Christmas day."

Fabe dramatically shook his head. "I done told you about fuckin' with all these chicks, man. When are…"

I interrupted his sermon. "Fuck all that! I need you to call Aaliyah and talk to her. She'll talk to you. I need to know where she is."

"I'm not getting in this middle of this bullshit, man." His tone was discerning. He was over me and my bullshit.

He stood and began to zip up his Billionaire Boys leather jacket like he was about to leave.

"Bro, listen," I said, meeting him where he stood. I changed my tone. I wanted him to see that I was his brother, not the ignorant ass dude that he was despising right then. "I need your help. It's a lot in it for you."

"Like that bank robbery?" He even had to laugh as he waited on the answer. His laughter rubbed me the wrong way.

No, I wasn't as successful with the robbery as I should have been. Yet, the way he mocked me was the same way Carlos had. These niggas was sleep on me. I woke up Carlos by putting a bullet in his head.

I had to wake my brother up to my level of power as well.

"The bank robbery went south, but I hit a better lick. But Aaliyah took the money when she bounced. That's why I need you to find her. You find her, I get my cash back, and its twenty–five thousand in it for you."

Honestly, I wasn't going to give him a gawd damn thing. But if that's what he needed to hear, so be it. Sure enough, he stopped his exit long enough to listen to me.

"Where you get that type of cash from?"

"I killed Carlos."

Fabe lost it. "The fuck?!"

He looked at me like I was a stranger. He even backed away from me in disgust.

"Are you fucking serious?!"

"I had to! He would have killed Moses because he didn't have the money to pay him back for that work!"

Fabe shook his head over and over again as he cupped his face. "Carlos wasn't that type of dude. He was your best friend."

"Exactly, so you don't know him like I did." Fabe was stuck. He didn't know what to believe, so I continued to beg. "Bro, please? I need you to find Aaliyah and my money."

"If you killed him to keep him off of Moses, why take the money?"

"Because it was there. The police would have just taken it. I can use it to take care of my family. Tabitha and kids need that. Even, Aaliyah and Nasiem. You too, man. You can take that money and open up that shop."

I had him. Finally, his eyes were done judging me. He was looking at me like I was his big brother.

He sighed and gave in. "Alright, man. I'll call her. I got you."

TABITHA

I was ignoring like the tenth phone call from Nas. I couldn't even get the bastard to look me in the eyes. Now suddenly he was blowing up my phone. He even sent me a text message, asking me to meet up with him somewhere so that we could talk.

He could kiss my ass. He'd ignored me for over a week while I went through pure hell. Now the motherfucker wanted to see me?

No.

I was lying in bed watching some reruns of *The Game*. Finally, life seemed to calm down a little bit. Moses was still unconscious, but his vital signs were good. The doctors planned to wake him up soon. Then I looked forward to him and Jaleesa being able to put their lives back together. Though it was hood as hell, those two loved each other. They just needed to figure it out.

I was even enjoying Jay's company. Because I had been spending so much time with the kids and at the hospital, I hadn't been able to take him up on the many invites to dinner that he'd given me. It was obvious that he liked me. It was shocking, but it felt good to be courted after fourteen years. I couldn't wait to see him, but I needed to get myself together.

Moses' death scare, DCFS, and Nas had brought a lot of things into perspective for me. I could no longer depend on Nas for anything. He didn't love me. He loved himself. He didn't even love his kids. So, it was time for me to love myself just as much as he loved himself. I needed to find a job, get back on my feet, and shake this feeling of defeat that Nas had continuously fed me over the years.

Yet, that feeling became unshakeable as Essence slunk into my room and crawled into bed with me. My eyebrows arched curiously because, not only had she been acting like she hated the world since she got home, she had never been one to lay under mommy.

She grabbed a pillow and literally curled up under my arm as I lay on my back waiting for the commercials to end.

She said, "Mommy," in such a frightened and timid tone that it scared the shit out of me. "I need to talk to you."

My heart immediately began to beat fast with anticipation. Your child needing to talk to you is never a good thing.

I remained calm, however. With the wrong tone, I would have scared her into silence, and I didn't want to do that.

I tried to remain as nonchalant as possible as I asked, "What's wrong, baby?"

"Promise you won't get mad and flip out."

Shit, I thought to myself as I rolled my eyes behind her head.

"I promise."

As soon as she opened her mouth, the cries forcing themselves out caused her voice to crack. "This boy at the home we had to stay in…"

Though I feared what she was trying to tell me, I encouraged her to go on when she hesitated. "Uh huh."

"He had sex with me."

It felt like the wind had been kicked out of me. Still, I remained calm, because I didn't want to freak her out. I wanted her to be comfortable enough to tell me everything. Kids were having sex young these days. Hell, I had given birth to her when I was only fourteen. It broke my heart, but I couldn't act like I didn't understand.

"What made you want to have sex, Essence?"

Immediately, she sat straight up. Finally, I could see the stress in her young face. Despite the developing breasts and hips that she hid under one of her father's shirts, she was still a very little girl. The immaturity and childlike fear was all over face and spilled out in tears.

"No," she cried. "I didn't have sex, mama. I didn't want to. He...he...he made me."

Then, she lost it. It's like she had been holding that in since she got home. She collapsed on top of me, buried her face in my chest, and literally wailed. I held her tightly as my own tears fell silently.

"What do you mean he made you, Essence? Tell me what happened."

"He told me that if I didn't, he would tell the supervisor that I did anyway, and then I wouldn't be able to go home. He said if I tried to fight him or scream, they would make me stay there forever for being alone with him."

My heart ached. My body cringed.

"Did he hit you?"

"No," she whined. "I just ... I didn't wanna do it mama, but I wanted to come home."

I bit my lip. There was so much anger in that bite that I could taste my own blood. I closed my eyes tightly as I fought the urge to explode. I had buried my anger for Nas, so that I could live and move on. Now, it came hurling back into my heart and mind.

I was beyond furious.

Yet, I remained calm on the outside and tried to be the best mother that I could be.

"It's going to be okay," I promised her. "Mommy will take care of it. Okay, baby?"

"It's not going to be okay!" She shrieked as she sat up again. "My period won't come on, mama!"

She was devastated. She was crying her slanted eyes out. God, I was heartbroken for my little girl. I couldn't even hide the remorse anymore. The hurt spilled from my eyes. When she saw my face, it was as if she wanted to die.

I wanted to die too.

AALIYAH

Fabe was calling for the fifth time that evening. I wanted to talk to him. He was the closest person to me, besides Nas. Considering what had went down though, I no longer knew if I could still trust him either.

Finally, I decided to answer. "You better not be calling me for your brother."

"I'm calling for me."

He actually sounded genuinely concerned, so I let my guard down. I laid back down under the bedding of the king sized bed in the Marriott. That is the only thing that I had been doing since I left the house. I didn't know what to do. I had a lot of hurt in my heart and a lot of cash in my pockets.

"He told me what happened," Fabe said. "Are you okay?"

No matter how hurt I was, I can't even deny how my body relaxed in the presence of his sympathy and concern.

"I guess," I answered.

"Where are you?"

"I don't want your brother to know…"

"Aaliyah, c'mon now," he fussed, interrupting me. "I wanna see you. I need to make sure you're okay."

Quietly, I pondered over the idea. I would have given anything to be held right then. His visit sounded like something that would make it all better, even if only temporarily. I had only had the comfort of my newborn. I needed somebody who could talk tell me that I wasn't tripping and that I had done the right thing.

Fabe sensed my hesitation. He smacked his lips. "Really, Aaliyah? I've been telling you to leave that nigga since you got with him. Why would I tell him where you were?"

He was right. Had I listened to his warnings in the past, I wouldn't be lying in bed with a purple ring around my neck.

"I'm at the Marriott on Sixty–Fifth and Cicero."

"I'm on my way."

He sounded like he was already in the car, so I believed that he would be there soon. I hadn't showered since I arrived at the hotel the morning before. I was too distraught to have the strength to do anything except feed my baby and use the bathroom. So, reluctantly I crawled from underneath the covers. On my way to the bathroom, I checked on Nasiem, who was fast asleep in the bassinet that I brought along with me from the house.

My body was so heavy with hurt as I prepared the shower and took off my sleep shirt. I couldn't believe that Nas had put his hands on me. He wasn't perfect, by any means. We'd argued countless times before. Never had he thought so little of me that he hit me, however. Never had his disrespect and dismissal of me been so blatant.

Yet, since he was capable of murder, I guess he had always been capable of anything.

My mind was so busy and my emotions were so fucked that I hadn't even eaten. So, after I got out of the shower, I could damn near smell the Italian Fiesta pizza on the other side of the door right before I heard a knock.

I wrapped the hotel towel around a body that was still dripping with hot water. I peeked out of the curtains. I couldn't deny how laying eyes on Fabe gave me a feeling of comfort that I hadn't felt in days.

I hid from the cold whipping winds behind the door as I opened it. Fabe rushed in with a cold so mighty that it sent arctic chills through my body.

"Shit, it's cold," I mumbled as I hurried and closed the door.

Fabe immediately put the pizza and brown bags down on the table. He turned to look at me. Instantly, I came towards him and fell into his arms. Though I buried my head in his chest, he picked my face up and began to examine me. He looked over my face and body. When he saw the bruises on my arms and around my neck, he bit his lip with sorrow and anger.

"I'm okay," I promised him.

His eyes burned into mine, silently telling me that he knew that I was lying.

I left him. I sat down on the bed and avoided him. At first, I thought his visit would be comforting. Now, I just felt stupid. He was standing there looking good and smelling good. He was standing there giving me the loving eyes that Nas never gave me. Compassion was oozing from him, when I never felt that from his brother. Yet, I denied him and stayed with a nigga that obviously never gave a fuck about me.

"You okay?"

I couldn't even lie to him, "Not really."

"How long you plan on staying at this hotel?"

"For a few days."

"And then?"

"I'm going to Houston."

Getting my mother out of that home would take a few days, but I had enough money to stay in that hotel for as long as it took. I kept those details away from Fabe, though. I didn't want anyone to know that I knew about that money or that Nas killed Carlos. I just wanted to leave and be free. I hated that it had to happen like this, but transferring my mother and being able to move her closer to her sister was the only ray of sunshine in the midst of this storm.

It almost made it all feel like it was worth it.

Fabe saw my weariness and put his arms around me. "I told you to leave that nigga."

When I lay my head on his shoulder, he began to soothingly rub my back. I fell into him. I relaxed into him. I only felt that protected when I was near him. Yet, for a year, I avoided being that close to him.

"I know," I told him with a sigh.

Being in his arms felt right. It felt real. It felt safe. It felt genuine. It felt totally opposite of Nas. It felt like falling in love over and over again with every minute he held me.

"But you loved him too much."

I had no response for that.

"Can I ask you a question?"

I dreaded what he would ask. I wasn't ready for some

deep ass conversation with him about how his brother wasn't shit and I dealt with it.

"Go ahead." However, he deserved that explanation if he wanted it. Hell, he had been more of a man to me emotionally than Nas ever had.

"Who is Nasiem's father?"

I wasn't expecting that question, though.

Anxiety came over me. For nine months, nobody questioned me. Nas didn't think twice. Fabe never once asked.

When I pondered over the answer and the embarrassment silenced me, Fabe asked, "You don't know, do you?"

The truth was I didn't. I had sex with Fabe and Nas days apart from each other. Nas never even considered using condoms. He told me that I was his and he was mine, so we didn't need them. Fabe, well, you can blame that recklessness on Remy Martin VSOP.

When my silence spoke of my guilt, anger seemed to overwhelm Fabe. He removed his arms from around me and slightly moved away from me. As soon as I saw that I had hurt him that much, I reached for him. I wrapped my arms him. As I did, my towel fell. For over a year, he looked at me like I was his everything. Now, he was looking at me like he hated me. I just wanted to fix it. I kissed him. Immaturely, I felt like that would make everything better. Surprisingly, he kissed me back. He didn't fight as I slipped my tongue into his mouth. When I felt his masculine big strong hands on my back, it was as if my pussy took over. I hadn't had sex in so long. My body knew what Fabe could do, and it wanted it. My heart knew that I had hurt his feelings by keeping his child away from him and thought that fucking him would fix it.

He acted like it did. He took over, taking advantage of me finally giving myself to him physically, just as he always wanted.

Fucking him would fix me too, if only for a moment. So, he used his weight against my body to force me down on the bed, and I invited him. I wrapped my petite arms around his strong neck and lost myself under him.

Resting against one elbow, he sucked my mouth as he unzipped his pants. My pussy oozed with anticipation of the dick that I recalled a little over nine months ago. I was eager. As we kissed, I reached for his dick, anxiously opened my legs, and brought it towards my opening. My pussy seemingly reached out to him as he slid into me. We both let out excited and amazed moans as his stiff long dick met my juicy insides.

"Shit," Fabe breathed into my ear. "Just like I remembered."

I was lost in the feeling. I was lost in the penetration. He didn't whale his dick into me selfish and aggressively. He took his time, found my spot, and massaged that motherfucker, just as he did the last time.

"I love you," softly swam into my ear in a deep whisper.

I gasped at the words. My eyes welled up when my heart felt the genuineness. My legs opened more, allowing him in deeper, fishing for him to say more.

I fought the urge to get too loud, in fear that Nasiem would awaken in his bassinet. But it was hard, because his dick was so hard and seemingly fucking my organs.

"Gawd damn," I groaned softly as Fabe lost his face in my neck.

He asked me, "You love me?" But didn't wait for an answer. He was seemingly fucking the love into my heart with purposeful attacks on my g spot. "Tell me you love me, baby."

I did. I always had. As sweat began to appear on the surface of our skin, I felt the love between us that had always been there, that we had always avoided.

Tears fell from eyes that were still sore from Nas' punches. "I love you too."

Nas

"I can't believe Carlos is gone, man. Are you okay?"

I looked up at Slim, one of the guys from the hood, trying to show as much remorse as I could.

Shit, I was super cool on the inside. I had been sitting in that hospital for days, imagining how I would spend that cash. I was ready to sell that bar to the highest bidder and chill while I made major purchases that I had only been able to previously dream of.

Yet, on the outside, I showed major remorse for the loss of my best friend. "Nah, not really," I told Slim as I lowered my head.

We were at The Black Room. The whole hood was there, mourning for Carlos and in support of Moses. I sat at the bar with many of Carlos' homeboys around me. They were showing me so much love because they figured this was hurting me the most since Carlos and I were so close.

I saw Caine enter the bar. Instantly, I got irritated. This nigga was so spooked about Tabitha spotting him. He was constantly calling me. He had even instilled that same fear in Nell and Lavell. They were all calling me asking what should be done. Each time I told them scary motherfuckers that the answer was to get rid of Tabitha, they bitched up.

Luckily, I was prepared to do it myself.

Caine approached me with the same fear that he'd had in his eyes since this issue with Tabitha came up. "What's going on, man?"

"Shit, bro," I answered as I took a long swig of the Remy from the glass I was clutching.

Everyone was drinking heavy. Carlos' death was a major loss. Many men were now out of product and a way to get money. They weren't only mourning Carlos. They were mourning their wallets as well.

I was just drinking to go along with it.

Though everyone had a fucked up disposition, Caine's blew me, because I knew that his had nothing to do with Carlos.

This robbery was on his mind heavy.

"Man, would you chill?" I made sure to keep it low. Music was blasting through the speakers. I leaned forward towards Caine as he leaned against the bar next to me.

"It ain't easy to chill," he didn't have a problem admitting. "You ain't the one facing time for no felony murder."

I actually laughed. "You act like you already got arrested. They ain't even investigating that shit."

Caine didn't find shit funny at all. "I just don't wanna go down for this. She saw me. She recognized me and started crying. She already popping off and goin' crazy on yo' ass. It's only a matter of time... I'm not going down for this shit."

Disgust filled my stare as it was obvious that he was insinuating that he wasn't taking the fall if it came to it. I could tell by the punk ass look in his eyes that he definitely was not going to take the fall alone.

I reached in my pocket for my cell. I called Tabitha a few times, knowing that she wouldn't answer. I had been trying to meet with her so that I could take care of this, but she wouldn't answer. I told her that we needed to talk about our family so that I could get her alone. However, talking we were not going to do. I had to take care of this shit before these stupid motherfuckers ruined my shit before I even got the chance to enjoy it.

CHAPTER FOURTEEN

Tabitha

By the time that I calmed Essence down and got her and Eric dressed and to my mom's, it was about two in the morning.

I stopped at Walgreens to buy a pregnancy test on the way to mom's house. As soon as we got there, I took Essence into the bathroom.

Five minutes later, we were both relieved that there was only one blue line. However, my only relief was for my child not having to face what I had at her age. She had another chance at doing motherhood the right way, though I was sure this situation would haunt her and make her hate her parents for life.

I had to talk to Nas. I had been ignoring him for days, but, as I got the kids settled, I replied to his text message, telling him to meet me at the house. He needed to know how far he had gone. I wanted him to know just how much his selfish acts had ruined our family. This shit had gone too far. Beyond fucking up my life, he had fucked up my daughter's.

Finally, he replied to me via text, telling me to meet him at the house in fifteen minutes.

"How are you going to take care of this?"

Despite it being in the middle of the night, my mama was wide awake. She was just as devastated and angry as I was. I was sure the poor lady was going to have a stroke, she was so angry. She was right on my heels, chasing after me, barefoot with a head bonnet and old nightgown on. She followed closely behind me as I left the guest room that Essence was sleeping in. I guess finding out that she wasn't pregnant gave her so much relief that she passed out.

"I'm going to go up to that home in the morning, mama."

"You need to be calling the police right now."

"I have to do that in the morning. It's been a long night. They are going to want to talk to Essence. She needs to rest."

"You need to file this report *now*, Tabitha!"

She was irritating the fuck out of me. I had enough on my mind. It was swimming with all kinds of realizations that were sending me further and further into hysteria. I didn't need my mother's nagging in addition to the bullshit.

I stopped suddenly. I spun around in the middle of the living room. She was following so closely behind me that she nearly ran into me.

"Mama! I *will* take care of it." She looked scornfully at my disrespectful tone, but I wasn't in the mood to be chastised. "I gotta go."

"Where are you going?"

"To talk to Nas."

"Why are you talking to him, Tabitha? He doesn't mean you or these kids any good. You need to forget that that bastard even exists."

"Mama, I gotta go."

I had to go. I had to get this shit off of my chest. The lies, the abortion, Aaliyah, their baby, taking my kids; he'd done so much and I just needed to know why. I needed to know why he had to go as far as putting my kids at risk just to prove a point. I wanted to know where the love had gone that fast that he didn't give a fuck about me so much that he was willing to go so far.

As promised, he was sitting in front of the house when I pulled up. I wondered why he didn't get out of his car as I climbed out and locked mine.

I approached his car feeling as if I was in the twilight zone. I wondered how this nigga could be so manipulative that he hid this evil side of him from me for so long. I hated him for what he had turned us into, what he turned me into. I felt hate inside of me that I never felt before. I despised him, when just a few months ago, I loved him too much to even imagine my days without him.

He rolled down the window as I approached his driver's side.

"Get in," he simply told me.

"Where are we going?"

"Let's just take a ride. I don't want to argue in front of the kids."

I rolled my eyes into the back of my head. Yet, I fought the venom that was threatening to come out of my mouth in words.

I knew him. Had I started going off right then, he would stubbornly pull off before I was able to say what I had to say.

"The kids aren't home. We can go inside."

Aaliyah

The insomnia caught up with me as soon as Fabe slid out of me and lay breathless next to me. We both laid beside one another completely silent. Only our heavy breathing could be heard. We hadn't fucked in damn near a year. Yet, we made up for it with hours upon hours of what felt like him sweetly punishing me with his dick for keeping the pussy away from him.

At first, I got anxious because he wasn't saying anything. I thought he was beginning to regret the love that we made. However, just as my heart began to beat heavy with disappointment, he rolled over and held me. Once again, I was lost in the love I felt in his arms and was asleep before I knew it.

For once, the sleep was restful. I wasn't worried about when Nas was coming home. I wasn't thinking about what I could do the next day to impress Nas, in order to ensure that I kept his interest. I didn't have to worry about anything.

Until Nasiem's cries woke me up.

I was jolted out of my sleep. I had been so comfortable that I nearly forgot that he was in the corner in the bassinet. The hotel curtains were night curtains, so I couldn't see the sun. Yet, I heard the birds chirping, so I knew that it had to be the early hours of the morning. I fought the darkness to feel around the bassinet and find Nasiem's pacifier. Angrily, he spit it out as soon as I put it in his mouth. He didn't want it. It was past time to feed him. Regretfully, I turned on the light, realizing that I had to fully wake up from such a good sleep.

That's when I noticed that the bed was empty. Where Fabe was once lying, beautifully naked, was an empty space. Only the impression of his head on the pillow was there. Curiously, I looked inside of the bathroom. There was only darkness in there. Nasiem started to cry. I picked him up from the bassinet while noticing that Fabe's coat was missing as well.

He was gone. Snatching my phone from the night stand, I dialed Fabe's number. It wasn't a mystery how he could have left without me knowing. I was knocked out. But I was irritated that he didn't even say goodbye.

Irritation turned to dread when my call went straight to voicemail. Every time I called – six times– it went straight to voicemail.

Dread turned to panic when I saw the closet door open. I jumped up so fast that Nasiem jumped in fright. Though he was still whimpering, I lay him in the bassinet as I went towards the closet. I flung the door wide open. Just as I suspected, the large garbage bags was gone! The money was gone!

"FUCK!"

I felt so fucking stupid. He was gone for good. I knew it. He hadn't mentioned anything about any money while he was there. Angry was not even the word to describe what I was feeling as I slammed the closet door. Nasiem burst out into a panicked cry then. So did I, as I slid down the wall and threw my arms over my head.

That was all that I had. Fabe knew that. He didn't even leave me a little, not even a dollar. I didn't have anywhere else to go. I didn't know what else to do. Obviously Fabe and Nas were working together and against me. If Fabe knew about the money, then he probably had an idea that I knew about the murder too.

I had no choice but to leave. I wasn't going to just sit there and wait for Nas to come next. I stood up to get myself together. As I looked in the mirror, with my baby's screams serenading me and Nas' bruises looking back at me, I stared at the reflection of my stupidity.

But I didn't have to continue to be so stupid for these niggas any more.

It was time.

I had to go.

I couldn't believe that things had gotten this bad. But when you refuse to learn the lessons that life is trying to teach you, it teaches you in a way that you cannot avoid. For so long, I worshipped the ground Nas walked on, knowing in the back of mind that he wasn't the one. And now, I was forced to leave, grow up, and take care of myself on my own.

Whether I liked it or not.

JALEESA

"Are you sure you want to do this, Jaleesa? We can fight this."

Standing up from the table at the lawyer's office, I knew that I was sure. I adjusted the blouse that I'd worn to the meeting and took my coat off of the back of my chair.

"I'm sure. In the end, I'll just get probation anyway. Why waste your time and mine?"

Sam, the lawyer I hired with Nas' money, looked disappointed. Yet, he smiled and nodded as if he respected my decision.

I told him that I would see him at court in a few weeks and hurried out of the office. During my meeting, Moses' mother had called and said that Moses was awake! He was groggy, but he asked for me, so I was in a hurry to get back there. I slipped on my leather blazer and hurried out of the office building.

For the first time in days, I had a feeling of joy. I felt good and like things were finally getting back to normal. Life wasn't perfect– not at all. Nevertheless, I had a lot of hope that everything was going to work out.

I practically ran towards my car that was parked half a block down the street.

Once inside of the car I called Tabitha back as I started the engine. She had called me at least a dozen times while I was in the meeting. She had also sent me a text message asking that I call her back as soon as possible.

I wasn't even paying attention when Tabitha answered. I cut her off with excitement as I whizzed through the traffic downtown. "Hey, Tabitha! I know! I'm on my way to the hospital now."

It was like she didn't even hear me. She sounded so out of it as she spoke to me. "Can you come by the house?"

"When? I need to get to the hospital right now. What's wrong?"

"Please, Jaleesa? It's really important."

When I heard the tears, I knew that Nas had done something. I shook my head in irritation and disappointment. I was so fucking sick of Nas and his bullshit. I couldn't understand why he just wouldn't leave that girl alone and let her live.

"Alright," I reluctantly told her. I didn't want to go, but she sounded like she really needed me. "I'm on my way."

She hung up without another word.

"This nigga irks my *soul*," I muttered through gritted teeth as I tossed the phone onto the passenger's seat.

I drove towards the expressway like a mad woman, with hate for Nas fueling my lead foot. Nas was like a thorn in my side. He was negatively affecting everyone's life around him. He was even affecting mine, and I wasn't even fucking him! He was like a virus; slowly eating away at the lives of all us with his inability to give a fuck about anybody else besides himself.

I thought that Tabitha was finally done with this nigga after this last major stunt that he pulled; but apparently not.

Finally, I arrived at Tabitha's and Nas's house, while being completely disgusted that, once again, my life was consumed by Nas or something to do with his ass. I needed to be at the hospital, not at their house consoling Tabitha after whatever stunt he pulled this time.

This better be real fucking important, I thought as I rang the bell. *She better not have called me over here because of some petty shit.*

I repeatedly moved my legs back and forth and stuffed my hands in my pockets to cope with the cold.

It was the beginning of winter, but it was already cold as fuck in Chicago. January was only two days away. That's when the real arctic air was going to blow through the city. As I waited for Tabitha to come to the door, I thought about New Year's Eve being the next day. Memories of all that I had been through came to mind, especially the events of the last few weeks. The memories were eerie, but I was happy to start this New Year with hopes of a much better tomorrow.

All of those hopes were lost when Tabitha finally answered the door looking like a walking car accident. Her blond hair was all over the place and hanging in her face. Her eyes were bloodshot red as they rained tears.

When I realized that the stains on her shirt were blood, I lost it. "Tabitha! Oh my God! Are you okay?!"

In response, she turned away from the door and began to mope as she walked away. I hurriedly followed her inside, closed the door, and followed closely behind her with a million questions.

"What happened?! Did Nas hit you?! What the hell is going on?!"

"That bitch ass nigga had the nerve to blame me for what happened to Essence!" She fussed in anger while making long, fast strides down the hall.

I was on her heels. I was damn near chasing her, confused as she rambled on and on and walked briskly through the house.

"He didn't care! I told him what happened to Essence, and he still didn't care!"

"Didn't care about what, Tabitha?"

She didn't even hear me. "I told him how much I wanted the baby. He just laughed. He dismissed my hurt like it didn't mean anything. He told me that I was overreacting. He said that this was *my* fault. Told me that if I was the ride or die bitch for my man that I was supposed to be, this wouldn't have happened to Essence."

As we entered the kitchen, I still didn't know what was going on. Yet it was obvious that Nas had finally gone too far. The look in Tabitha's eyes was angrier than I had ever seen before.

She was possessed with fury.

Tabitha was still rambling on and crying, nervously running her fingers through her hair.

She sounded like a crazy person. "And do you know what he had the nerve to say?" Her face lost all sanity as she recalled it in her mind. "He said that if Essence wasn't such a hoe like her mother, maybe this wouldn't have happened to her."

  I cringed. Nas' words even hurt *my* feelings as I leaned against the island in the kitchen. "Tabitha, what…"

  I stopped mid–sentence when my eyes fell upon the scene on the floor near the back door.

  I gasped so loud that it bounced off of the walls. "Tabitha! What did you do?!"

Nas was lying on the floor in a pool of blood. He was on his stomach. It was obvious that he was dead. I was shocked by the sight of his body and the blood all over the walls. I then looked into Tabitha's eyes, which showed no remorse; only fear of what would now happen to her because of what she had done.

I stood frozen in place, gaping at Nas' lifeless body with my mouth ajar in pure shock. "How long has he been lying there?"

Tabitha shrugged her shoulders with weary eyes. She looked just as thirteen as Essence was. "I don't know. A few hours."

When she saw that I had the same fear, she began to justify what she had done through hysterical screams. "He ruined my baby! He ruined me, Jaleesa! And he didn't even care. He didn't even care!!"

I threw my arms around her. I could imagine Nas' blood seeping into the fabric of my jacket as it pressed against Tabitha's shirt. As I held her, she rocked back and forth in agony.

"I ... I didn't mean to. I just got so mad. I was *so* mad..." Her words trailed off in wails of sorrow and fear.

Suddenly, she released me and reached for the cell phone that sat on the counter.

"What are you doing?"

When she answered, "Calling 9-1-1," I instinctively rushed towards her and snatched the cell phone away.

"No," I told her. "Don't call the police."

It just didn't seem right to call them. I imagined them showing up at this scene and hauling her away in handcuffs. I had just taken a charge because of the inconsiderateness of a nigga. I wasn't about to allow Tabitha to do the same.

"I have to call the police, Jaleesa. He's dead."

Even though she knew that it was the right thing to do, she looked so scared for what would happen to her when she did call them. When I imagined her being handcuffed and hauled away, it just didn't feel fair. She didn't deserve it. Seeing Nas' body bleeding out and lifeless, *that* felt fair. Nas had taken every opportunity to ruin her life. She had fought him tooth and nail not to allow him too. Yet, he insisted on fucking with her because she had sense enough to leave him. Even in death, he was threatening to ruin her life.

"Let's just take care of it," I told her as I took off my coat.

She looked at me like I was crazy. "Take care of it? What do mean?"

"We can dump his body somewhere. Let the police find him." Though I sounded crazy even to myself as I said it, it sounded way better than calling the police. "Shit, they would think anything could have happened to him. But you should not have to spend the rest of your life in jail for this nigga. Do you want to lose your kids?"

I was so sincere that my eyes began to tear up with sincerity.

Tabitha couldn't answer me. Her eyes were beady with anxiety. They darted back and forth from me, to Nas, and to the cell phone. She was sweating profusely. She kept opening her mouth, but nothing would come out.

So, I answered for her. "Where is the bleach?"

For a few seconds, Tabitha just stood there. She was confused and lost. I let her stand there as I took off my shoes and socks and threw them into the hallway. I rolled up my jeans. Then I left her standing there as I started to run hot water in the sink and began to search the cabinets for cleaning products.

It was outlandish, but letting this nigga continue to fuck up her life was even more outlandish. He was an asshole that intentionally fucked up everything in his path. She'd given herself loyally to him, and he gave her back hate. He didn't have any remorse, not even for his children. My own household had suffered because Moses was loyal to this nigga. Moses was sitting in the hospital with a shit bag attached to him, which he would probably have to wear for the rest of his life, because of his loyalty to this nigga.

Nas had used everyone's loyalty around him and selfishly never returned it.

He deserved whatever Tabitha had done to him in that kitchen.

As Tabitha finally appeared next to me, wearing a pair of plastic gloves and handing me a bottle of bleach, I knew that she felt the same.

THE END

OTHER TITLES BY JESSICA N. WATKINS:

Secrets of a Side Bitch

Secrets of a Side Bitch 2

Secrets of a Side Bitch 3

Good Girls Ain't No Fun

Text the keyword "Jessica" to 25827 to sign up for text message alerts for future book releases by Jessica N. Watkins.

JOIN JESSICA N. WATKINS ONLINE:

www.Jessica-N-Watkins.com

http://www.facebook.com/authorjwatkins

http://www.facebook.com/groups/femistryfans

http://www.twitter.com/authorjwatkins

Made in the USA
Middletown, DE
26 May 2022

66288960R00149